A SMALL-TOWN TEMPTATION

BY
TERRY McLAUGHLIN

First published in Great Britain 2010
Harlequin Mills & Boon Limited,
Eton House, 18-24 Paradise Road, Richmond, Surrey TW9 1SR

© Teresa A McLaughlin 2008

ISBN: 978 0 263 87999 5

23-0910

Harlequin Mills & Boon policy is to use papers that are natural, renewable and recyclable products and made from wood grown in sustainable forests. The logging and manufacturing processes conform to the legal environmental regulations of the country of origin.

Printed and bound in Spain
by Litografia Rosés S.A., Barcelona

Terry McLaughlin spent a dozen years teaching a variety of subjects, including anthropology, music appreciation, English, drafting, drama and history, to a variety of students from kindergarten to college before she discovered romance novels and fell in love with love stories. When she's not reading and writing, she enjoys travelling and dreaming up house and garden improvement projects (although most of those dreams don't come true). Terry lives with her husband in Northern California on a tiny ranch in the redwoods. Visit her at www.terrymclaughlin.com.

For Rob

CHAPTER ONE

JACK MAGUIRE WOULDN'T BE needing a second look to confirm the rumor: Charlie Keene was a woman who could give a man hell. She stood a dozen yards away, her muddy boots planted at the edge of Earl Sawyer's gravel yard, flaring up like a pint-size serpent to poke a pointy finger at his gut. And if that image wasn't enough of a giveaway, all a guy had to do was listen. She hissed and spat in a fire-and-brimstone vocabulary, providing Sawyer with an impressive preview of everlasting damnation.

The plant operator who'd pointed out Charlie and Earl climbed back on his loader. Jack waved his thanks and leaned against his rental sedan to enjoy the show. Sawyer tried to duck out of the fight with a feint to the left, but Charlie cut off his escape with some fast footwork and another round of curses.

One side of Jack's mouth twisted in a lopsided grin. He'd enjoy doing a little ducking and weaving of his own before he delivered the knockout punch.

Before he put her out of business.

Sawyer laughed at something Charlie said and shook his head. She sure was a cute little thing, an inch or two over five feet and close to ninety pounds of atomic energy bundled up in workman's coveralls. Her firecracker hair exploded out the back of her visored work cap, and her square, stubborn chin shoved up toward Sawyer's grizzled beard. Not Jack's usual taste in women, perhaps—too much spice in her attitude, not enough sugar in her shape—but kind of appealing, in a handle-at-your-own-risk kind of way.

Jack always had enjoyed the adrenaline rush of a calculated risk. His smile spread with one part anticipation and three parts pure male speculation. It looked like this business trip up the coast from San Francisco might be more interesting than he'd figured.

Charlie tossed up her hands with a frustrated growl, shot Sawyer one final, lethal glare and stomped toward the battered Keene Concrete pickup truck parked near Jack's car. Her pretty mouth moved in a muttered litany of maledictions as she rammed her hands into her mud-spattered coverall pockets and kicked at a loose piece of cobble in her path.

She stumbled over another when she noticed Jack grinning at her, and she faltered, just for a moment, while a charming blush flooded her cheeks. And then her eyes—Jack thought they might be as dark and gray as the wet gravel—narrowed to slits, and a touch of the heat she'd been directing at Sawyer snapped across the yard and sizzled right through him.

Jack rubbed a fist over his heart. God almighty, the lady could torch the countryside with that flamethrower stare of hers. Probably came in handy for keeping badass drivers and fresh-handed boyfriends in line. He worked up another grin, just to show he wasn't completely charred, while she yanked her abused pickup's door open, climbed inside and peeled out of the yard, spitting gravel in her wake.

"Maguire?" Sawyer sloshed through a gravel-lined puddle, one work-roughened hand outstretched to take Jack's. "Jackson Maguire?"

"That's right."

"Earl Sawyer." The wiry man had a grip like a vise on a machinist's bench. "Welcome to BayRock. Understand you represent some folks who're looking to get a piece of the Carnelian Cove ready-mix business, Mr. Maguire."

"Folks call me Jack." He paused to watch a mixer truck pull under the concrete batch plant and stop, idling for the next load. The driver climbed down from the cab and headed for the office, juggling his clipboard as he lit a cigarette. "Looks like a busy place."

"Can be, sometimes." Sawyer nodded with muted pride and satisfaction at a loader dumping a scoop of sand into the bed of a customer's pickup truck.

Jack took the opportunity to scan the yard, quickly assessing the equipment and layout at Sawyer's BayRock Enterprises. A few streaks of rust edged the seams of the batch plant, and the dozen assorted loading and delivery trucks were mostly older models, but everything appeared to be operational and in good repair. To the north, near the gunmetal-gray ripples of the Ransom River, conveyor belts dribbled freshly screened material over neat cones of sand and gravel, and a vast, misshapen mound of river run hulked beneath February's sullen, fog-dampened sky.

It was the river run Jack's employer had an interest

in acquiring—tens of thousands of cubic yards of rough material waiting to be sifted into gravel gold. That, and the permit to scrape still more sand and gravel from the river's bars when the water level fell in the summer.

Sawyer hitched his pants up an inch over hips as spare and angular as the rest of his build. "Got a big pour at the tribal casino today."

"Saw some pier forms going up for a bridge just south of here," said Jack. "You doing that, too?"

Jack already knew the answer. The bridge job was Keene Concrete's, just like most of the government projects in the area. Which was surprising, considering Sawyer's outfit was the only one in town with a union contract.

Jack didn't like surprises. That was one reason he'd informed his regional manager that he was making the trip north to check out the situation for himself.

"We couldn't have handled a bridge pour today," said Sawyer with a shrug. "We've got our hands full with the casino."

"How many yards?"

"Plenty." Sawyer squinted at the mixer truck spinning its drum as material fell from the batch plant's weigh hopper. "Had to rent a couple of trucks from our competitor to handle it."

"Keene Concrete?"

"Yep." Sawyer's measuring gaze settled back on Jack's face. "It's just the two of us around here."

Jack followed Sawyer across the yard, pausing to let a loader rumble past and dump a scoop of pea gravel into the feeder bin at the base of the batch plant's conveyor belt.

"Pretty wet winters here, I s'pose," said Jack. "Projects get backed up to spring?"

"A few." Sawyer shrugged away the region's long, gray rainy season. "If a fellow was interested in buying a place like this one, it might be a good time to get a deal cooking, so he could get in on the early summer rush."

"Might be," said Jack with a noncommittal smile.

Sawyer paused outside his squat concrete-block office building with his hand on the doorknob. "Just thought I should mention I've already got one offer on the table. Figured I'd take it."

Jack nodded. He already knew about the offer, too. "Smart move," he said, "since you probably figured you wouldn't get another one."

"Told the other party I'd take it, too."

"No problem." Jack shoved his hands into his pockets. "And no harm in listening to what I've got to say."

"Just wanted to be up front about the situation here."

"Being up front is always good business."

Sawyer continued to study Jack with that squinty-eyed stare for another long moment and then twisted the knob and motioned him inside. "I'll keep that in mind."

CHARLIE CHARGED INTO THE cramped reception area of the office trailer at Keene Concrete twenty minutes later and slammed the door shut behind her. The fiberboard paneling on the walls vibrated in sympathy, and fine gray cement dust whirled in eddies around her feet. On the cork display board hanging over the scarred laminate counter, an oversize aerial photo of the Ransom River swung and settled back into place.

"Shit," she muttered. Here she was, scrambling to keep the place from coming apart at the seams while her brainless younger brother made a hash of today's schedule by renting out two of their trucks. She'd harassed the shop mechanic to get a wheezing mixer ready to roll in record time, and then had spent the morning making deliveries herself. Her back ached, her head throbbed and her stomach was begging for the take-out breakfast grown stone-cold on her desk. "Shit, shit, *shit*."

"Come on, Charlie," said Gus Guthrie, Keene's ancient dispatcher. He tilted back on his chair's casters and balanced his massive coffee mug on one of his spindly thighs. "Why don't you tell us how you really feel?"

She pointed a warning finger. "I don't want to talk about it."

"Fine by me." He aimed his thumb toward the phone on his massive metal desk. "Red Simpson's on line two. Doesn't think he should have to pay the standing time on the Maple Street job last month."

"Then he should've had his crew finish up the forms before we showed up with the truck."

Some of her customers kept forgetting they weren't the only ones with a clock ticking on payroll expenses. Keeping a mixer truck idling at the curb while a construction crew got ready for a concrete pour meant the driver was getting paid for sitting in his cab, listening to the radio or flipping through a magazine—and that his truck was unavailable for making other deliveries and selling more product.

Argumentative customers, botched delivery schedules, increasing fuel prices, union contract negotiations…

Charlie rubbed her forehead and tried to remember if the king-size aspirin bottle in her lower-left desk drawer had already run to empty. "I'll take the call."

"Figured you might." He lifted the giant mug to his lips and sipped one of the half dozen coffees he drank daily. "Figured you might be primed to deal with your good buddy Red right about now."

"Now, Gus." She spared him a nasty smile as she punched at the blinking light on the phone panel. "You know the customer's always right."

Gus humphed and slurped more coffee. "Unless he's dumber than dirt."

She took a deep breath and tamped down her anger over the morning's scene at BayRock. Dealing with Red was going to hitch her blood pressure into the danger zone as it was. "Hey, Red," she said in a neutral voice. "How's it going?"

She paced the length of the counter and back again as Red blasted her for adding her driver's extra time on the site to his bill. Red was one of those contractors who worked a little too close to the edge, shaving his costs by trying to shift some of his risks onto his subcontractors and suppliers. Better to force Charlie to pay her driver to wait on the job than to pay his own crew to wait for the truck to arrive.

She and Red had gone this round before. They'd likely go it again. Red never seemed to figure out how hard he could push his crew or how long he could push the odds. But the talk around town was his twin daughters were going to need braces to fix those twisted teeth, and Red was going to need every penny he could squeeze out of every angle if he was going to pay for them.

"I can take off thirty minutes," said Charlie. "And that's my final offer."

"Thirty minutes? Hell, just last week Buzz wasn't here any longer than ten. How come you get to charge for overtime, and I don't get a break for under?"

"Thirty, Red. Take it or leave it."

"Your old man would have listened to reason. Mitch knew how to run a fair business."

Charlie's fingers tightened on the receiver. "Yeah, that's right," she said, her voice sounding much steadier than she felt at the moment. "My father would have listened. And then he would have offered exactly the same kind of deal I've given you."

She paused for a moment to control her temper. "I listened, too, Red. I listened in on plenty of conversations just like this one when he was alive—enough to know what I'm doing."

Red growled and muttered his standard filth about women in the construction business. "Guess I'll be calling BayRock when I get that Hawthorne job."

"Guess you might."

They both knew it was a bluff. Earl Sawyer probably wouldn't let Red add any charges to his BayRock account right now, since Earl didn't have Charlie's patience with delinquent payments. "Thirty," she said again.

Red ranted a while longer before disconnecting. Charlie slowly, carefully lowered the receiver into its cradle, her fingers shaking. The comment about her father had stung. "Comparing that man to dirt does dirt a disservice."

"Well," said Gus with a sympathetic shrug, "we'll make up the difference on the Hawthorne pour."

"That job bid already?" Charlie checked her watch. Pinch-hitting as a driver had thrown her day out of whack. "Who got it?"

Gus's homely face cracked with a wide grin. "Bradford."

"*Yes.*" She punched the counter with her fist, already figuring the profit in her head. Bradford Industries was efficient, cooperative, paid on time and was a rock-solid customer. If Bradford got the bid, Keene would do the pour. A big one, with plenty of deep, wide surface area and a minimum of the kind of detail work that kept trucks idling while pump operators and concrete finishers filled and smoothed every nook and cranny.

"David seems happy enough about the news," said Gus.

"Yeah. Right."

Charlie regretted the sarcastic remark the moment it flew from her mouth. Her younger brother meant well, most of the time. Well, some of the time, anyway, but his heart simply wasn't committed to the family business. Never had been, though their father had struggled for years to find some aspect of Keene Concrete that might engage his only son's interest. Nothing had worked.

David claimed he had a talent for metal sculpting and ambitions to make his mark in the art world, but he'd sold only two pieces and hadn't completed the application for the San Francisco art academy he hoped to attend. Instead, he'd complained his responsibilities were holding him back, and he'd launched a campaign to sell the business the day after they'd put their father in the ground, two long and difficult years ago.

Charlie sighed. "Is he in his office?"

"Yep." Gus stared at the mug in his hands. "Been on the phone most of the morning."

"Could be woman trouble." David hadn't yet figured out the math: dating more than one woman at a time didn't mean his problems would multiply, it meant they'd increase at exponential rates.

"Yep." Gus turned the mug in one circle, and then another. "Could be."

Watching Gus spin that mug knotted up Charlie's guts. She knew her dispatcher was aware of the arguments behind the scenes. David had stormed out of the office more than once lately, threatening to force the issue. To force her to sell.

Bad enough her employees had to deal with a female boss who, at twenty-nine, was younger than most of them. Bad enough they had to deal with the rigors of the job itself, with the long, grueling hours when the weather cooperated and the uncertain hours when it didn't. She didn't want them to have to worry about whether they'd keep their jobs on top of all that.

There were few secrets in a town the size of Carnelian Cove, and no secrets when it came to Keene family business, thanks to David's indiscretion. Their father had split the company stock equally among his three heirs: his wife, his son and his daughter. Once David convinced their mother to let him put it up for sale, Keene Concrete would go to the highest bidder, and Charlie would likely be looking for another steady job along with some of her current employees.

Unless she could convince both her mother and David to help her buy BayRock, which might provide her mother with enough security to soothe her worries and give David a big enough raise to either purchase his loyalty or pay for his tuition. And unless she could make Keene Concrete too big for the hungry conglomerates down south to swallow without getting a bad case of heartburn.

Just last week she'd heard that a Continental Construction rep had been prowling among the sand and gravel suppliers in the neighboring county. That was entirely too close for comfort.

She turned her back on the reception counter and started down the short hall that led to the back offices and storage areas. Avoiding the bookkeeper's attempt to flag her down and the view of her messy desk piled high with invoices and mail, she stopped at David's door. It was closed, as usual. She stared at the shiny new brass name plate covering the lettering still visible in the wood below: Mitch Keene, Owner.

Not President or CEO, like the puffed-up titles on David's nameplate. *Owner.* Their father had been a plain, quiet man, with a plain, quiet pride in the business he'd built from one delivery truck and a two-year lease on a river bar. He'd taken a simple satisfaction in what he'd been able to provide for his family and offer to his employees, and a quiet pleasure in what he'd contributed to his community. Keene Concrete had earned a reputation for solid dealing to match the solid foundations it poured.

How could David want to auction off that legacy?

She sucked in a deep breath, raised her hand, prayed for patience and knocked on the door.

"Yeah?"

"It's me," said Charlie. "I'm coming in."

CHAPTER TWO

CHARLIE IGNORED DAVID'S SCOWL as she dropped into one of his plush visitors' chairs.

"Why don't you ever make 'coming in' a question instead of a fact?" he asked.

"Because it saves time."

He leaned back in his tall leather swivel chair and bounced the eraser end of a freshly sharpened pencil against his tidy desk calendar. The weak winter sun sneaking through the window behind him picked out strands of copper in his well-mannered chestnut hair, a head of hair that Charlie, with her out-of-control carrot curls, never ceased to envy. Just as she never ceased to envy the way his clothes neatly outlined his long, rangy frame, while hers simply buried what little there was of her figure.

Today he wore a dress shirt and tie, and she spied a new leather jacket hanging from the mirrored wall rack behind him. "Going somewhere?" she asked.

"Already been." His expression brightened with the trace of a smile. "I stopped by that new hotel going up south of the marina—you know, Quinn's job. He liked my sketches. He's going to show them to the architect, see if he might be interested in using my design for the water feature near the entrance."

Charlie didn't respond to David's smile with one of her own. Quinn was one of the busiest contractors in Carnelian Cove, a dour, hard-working man who probably didn't appreciate David traipsing around his job site, artwork in hand.

Her brother cleared his throat, and then he flipped the pencil in his hand and drew a box around a calendar item. "And then I've got a business appointment."

"Here?"

Obviously annoyed, he flicked an impatient glance in her direction. "This is a place of business."

"Yeah. Right." She tossed her chin at the jacket. "Where did you get that?"

"The city." He took a deep breath and blew it out with a martyred sigh. "Is that why you barged in here? To comment on my wardrobe?"

Charlie shifted forward. "You loaned out two of our trucks this morning."

He shrugged. "Earl called me at home last night and asked for them."

And she'd just made sure Earl would never pull that stunt again. "How many times have I told you not to make a move without checking with Gus first?"

David jammed the pencil into a bristling mass of writing tools corralled in a slick chrome cup. "Gus isn't the boss around here."

"He's the dispatcher, and when it comes to which truck goes where, and when, that's more important than whose name is on whose check."

"Damn it, Charlie—"

"Just shut up and listen, for once." She came out of her chair, slapped her hands on his desk and leaned over him. "I let you declare yourself president of Keene Concrete because I hoped it would change your attitude. It's time for you to start acting like you give a damn what happens to it."

"Don't you lecture me."

"Someone's got to."

He clenched his jaw, and she knew he wouldn't budge on this. Not today, anyway.

"Aw, hell." She spun away and moved to the window to stare at the wide, gravel-coated yard. Outside, Buzz pulled beneath the batch plant to load his truck for the preschool playground job, and Lenny rumbled by in the transfer with sixteen yards of sand headed for Delores Fregoso's riding arena.

"Don't make this harder than it has to be," she said in a near whisper. "Don't sabotage this. Please."

"I'm not sabotaging anything. I'm trying to find a way for all of us to get what we want. All of us, Charlie. Not just you."

She turned as he stood to pull his jacket off its hanger. "There are going to be some changes around here," he said. "Whether you like them or not."

TWO HOURS LATER, CHARLIE leaned back in her chair with a groan that morphed into a yawn. Time for another dose of caffeine. She tugged her coffee mug from under a stack of Department of Motor Vehicles forms and trudged toward the reception area. Around the corner, she heard a deep murmur followed by Gus's wheezy chuckle. Someone was busy charming her dispatcher. Someone with a syrupy Southern drawl in his smooth, low-pitched voice.

That stranger, the guy who'd been staring at her in Earl's gravel yard that morning. He leaned against the counter as if he'd been born with the laminate attached at the hip. His jeans were white at the seams, poised on the edge between ragged and stylish, his wool shirt faded enough to show some use but soft enough to advertise its pedigree. The outfit may have said everyday working guy, but she suspected the labels whispered weekend leisure wear.

He straightened and turned to face her, and she couldn't help but stare at the flesh and blood embodiment of every bittersweet promise and mortifying low point in her brief and forgettable dating career. There was the lean-muscled build of that high school wrestler, the one who'd been such a perfect fit during a long, slow number at the homecoming dance—the one who'd lost his dinner all over her first formal gown. There was the wavy, dark blond hair of that sexy grad student, the one who'd whisked her away for her first taste of grown-up excitement—the one who'd ducked out in the middle of a double date, doubling her mortification. There were the dark blue, crinkle-cornered eyes of the man who'd been her first serious love affair, the one who'd said he was serious about her, too—the one who'd stood her up for Christmas dinner at her parents' house four years ago.

And then the lean, sexy, blue-eyed stranger standing at her counter smiled, and his tanned skin stretched and molded in a wonderful combination of sharp cheekbones and square jaw and deeply carved grooves far too manly to pass for dimples. Okay, so the grooves were something new. And that look in his eyes that was making her stomach twist in a breath-robbing knot—no one's eyes had ever looked at her in quite that way before. As if they were peeling away her clothes and counting every freckle on the skin underneath.

She hated it when guys made her stomach knot up. It gave her heartburn.

Gus gestured with his coffee mug. "This here's Jackson Maguire, Charlie. He says he has an appointment with David."

Jackson Maguire thrust his hand forward. "Call me Jack."

She placed her hand in his, noting a healing nick on his thumb and the calluses rubbing against her palm. This was a man who used his hands for work, but the careful weight of his grip gave the impression of precise and practiced manners. An interesting man, this Call-Me-Jack Maguire. A man of intriguing contrasts and textures.

"Charlie Keene," she said, and then she pulled her hand from his and shoved it into her pocket, where it would be safe.

"Do you know when David's due back?" Gus asked her.

"He mentioned he had an appointment," she said, "but all I know is that it was set for sometime after lunch."

"I'm afraid I'm early," said Jack. "Y'all just go about your business, now. Never mind me. Gus, here, is keeping me plenty entertained, in between all those phone calls he handles so well."

Maguire winked at her. A slow burn kindled in her

cheeks, and she knew she'd soon be wearing the same blush he'd seen on her that morning. She covered it with a nod and a shuffle to the coffeemaker.

"Pretty busy place here, even in the afternoon," Maguire rambled on in his amiable way. "Trucks coming and going, steady as can be. I would have thought things might slow down some after the morning pours, especially in a town this size. I s'pose most of the traffic must involve gravel deliveries about this time of day."

She couldn't tell if he was simply making conversation or prying into her business affairs. There was something about the sly specificity of his questions—wrapped up in that "aw, shucks" delivery—that tickled the hairs on the back of her neck.

She turned with a shrug. "Some," she said.

"Some." His mouth turned up at one corner. "But not all."

"Nope."

Behind her, Gus sputtered through a strangled cough.

Maguire's grooves deepened. "Now, that's as concise, and yet at the same time, as eloquent an answer as I think I've ever heard."

"And I imagine you've heard all kinds," she said.

That crooked smile of his seemed to tweak and tease at each of his features before coming to rest in his eyes. Quite a trick. Her stomach was knotting up so tight she wondered if she'd be able to make it back to her office without getting a cramp.

David sauntered in through the office door. He took one look at Maguire, a second at Charlie, and his golfer's tan faded several shades.

Charlie narrowed her eyes. "David?"

"David Keene?" asked Maguire, although it was obvious he already knew the answer.

At David's hesitant and guilty-looking acknowledgment, Maguire extended his hand. "Jack Maguire," he announced. And then he paused and flashed yet another grin in her direction. "From Continental Construction."

Continental. Charlie's mug clattered down on the counter, and coffee sloshed over the rim. *Oh God oh God oh God.*

Maguire tsked at the spilled coffee as he followed David through the doorway to the back offices.

That damn, cocky grin. The stomach-knotting trademark of the man who had appeared out of nowhere, the one who could get her juices flowing with his easy talk and his rough hands—the one who could hurt her more than any other man had ever hurt her in her life.

The hell he could.

Charlie snapped out of panic mode and strode down the hall after them. David's *business appointment* was about to get his agenda adjusted.

JACK TOOK ONE OF THE visitors' chairs in David Keene's office and crossed an ankle over a knee. He figured he had about ten seconds before David's sister came barging in.

Five seconds later the office door swung open so hard it bounced off the baseboard spring and closed behind her with a *smack*. His guess had been off. Charlie Keene moved fast when she was in a temper.

"Don't let me disturb you," she said as she dragged the

other chair behind David's desk—to the administrative side of the small room—and tucked it under an anemic-looking potted palm. "Go right ahead and discuss what it was you wanted to discuss. Just ignore the co-owner in the corner."

She dropped into her seat and slouched with her arms folded across her nearly flat chest, a fraudulent smile thinning her lips.

David leaned back with a sigh. "You'll have to forgive my sister, Jack. She tends to forget her manners when she walks through that door."

Jack glanced at the woman glaring at him from her spot beneath the greenery. One scrawny frond brushed against her cheek, and she swatted it out of the way. "There's nothing to forgive," he said. "I'm perfectly capable of ignoring something, or someone, I'm told to ignore. Discretion is an important social skill, along with manners and the like."

He hadn't thought it was possible for Charlie's expression to get any more hostile, but he'd guessed wrong about that, too.

He stifled a smile, figuring it would be like setting a torch to a short fuse. Except for his slight miscalculations about her temperament, so far Ms. Charlene Elizabeth Keene was living up to her reputation and his research. Which meant the rest of what he'd discovered was probably true—the lady had a clever enough brain and a strong enough back to carry most of the load at Keene Concrete.

He knew she was after Sawyer's ready-mix company, too, scheming to ease her competitor into an early retirement and secure her company's future in Carnelian Cove. Jack wondered how quickly she might blast through her family complications once she learned the purpose of this visit. Soon, he hoped. He relished the challenge of a tough, resourceful adversary.

Her brother cleared his throat, and Jack realized he'd been staring. David swiveled his chair a few degrees, attempting to cut Charlie out of the conversation. "I hope you had a nice trip north."

"I did at that." Jack nodded. "Enjoyed the scenery on the way in from the airport. Nice country you've got around here." That was an understatement—the views were spectacular. Massive redwoods crowding the pavement's edge, twisted cypress hugging cliffs dashed with sea spray. Mountains carpeted in thick forests and rolling pastures dotted with fat dairy cows. Rivers so clear he was tempted to pull over and toss in a lure.

"We like it." David squeezed a pencil with white-knuckled fingers. "The tourists do, too. We get plenty of visitors. In the summer, when the weather gets nicer."

Jack nodded. "That would bring 'em out, all right."

Charlie shifted in her seat and rolled her eyes toward the ceiling. Jack had to give her points for keeping her mouth shut.

"I'm glad you could make it up here," said David. "I was hoping you'd be able to check out the situation for yourself."

"That's why I'm here." Jack gave him a wide smile. "To check out the situation."

David sketched a zigzag in one corner of his desk blotter. "I hear you stopped by Sawyer's yard this morning."

"I did, yes." Jack's smile stayed in place. "Part of the situation, don't you think?"

"But not an important one," said David. "Well, not in a… What I mean is, he's retiring, and…" He cleared his throat again. "There won't be any competition around here once he does. Retire, I mean."

"Continental's not worried about a little competition," said Charlie. She leaned forward, her hands on her knees. "Isn't that right, Mr. Maguire?"

"Please," said Jack as he leaned more comfortably against the back of his chair, "call me Jack."

"In fact," said Charlie, ignoring his request, "Continental doesn't care which ready-mix outfit it buys. BayRock or Keene Concrete—it doesn't matter at all, not in the end. It's a buyer's market here in Carnelian Cove, isn't it, Mr. Maguire?"

Jack spread his hands. "It would sure be nice to think so, especially if a fellow were on a shopping trip."

David sent his sister a murderous look. "Be that as it may, I'm sure Continental will want to consider getting the best value for its money in the Cove—in the local market."

"The best value? The local market?" Charlie stood and shoved the palm frond out of her way. "If Continental buys Keene Concrete, Earl won't be able to sell his outfit to anyone, and there go his retirement plans—everything he's worked so hard for all these years. If Continental buys BayRock, it'll cut the price of concrete below cost and bleed us into bankruptcy in a matter of months."

She rested a hand on her brother's shoulder. "Either way, Mr. Maguire's bosses aren't going to have any competition in Carnelian Cove." She tilted her head to the side and leveled her dark gray eyes on Jack's. "Isn't that right, Mr. Maguire?"

"It's Jack." God almighty, going a round or two with this woman was going to be a whole lot of fun. Not to mention that the more he looked at her, the more he wanted to keep right on looking at her. She'd pulled off her cap, and that thick, springy hair seemed to wave and wind around her shoulders with a will of its own. Her wide mouth softened into a pillowy curve during those rare moments she wasn't frowning or cursing or arguing. And the crackling intelligence in her smoky eyes made it difficult for him to tug his gaze from hers.

"Well now, David." Jack set his foot on the ground and rose from his chair with a friendly smile. "I'd like that look at your operation you promised, if you don't mind."

CHAPTER THREE

JACK SWUNG HIS GARMENT bag over his shoulder later that afternoon and paused to admire the gaily colored Victorian houses standing shoulder-to-shoulder in their postcard pose along Oyster Lane. Stretched atop the rail of a white picket fence, a fat tabby spared him a crotchety meow before shifting its attention to the gulls overhead. The scents of salt-crusted docks, wood smoke and early hyacinths blended in the offshore breeze, a perfume that was Carnelian Cove's own.

An interesting town, he thought, packed with the kind of character that came with several different interests nurtured in relative isolation. Fishermen and artists, lumberjacks and university professors, dairy farmers and silversmiths—all rubbing up against each other in an eclectic collection of shops and neighborhoods that appeared to predate the concept of zoning restrictions. Untidy and unexpected, and charming in an offbeat way.

Sort of like the carved driftwood sign hanging from a reproduction London gaslight: Villa Veneto Bed and Breakfast.

He wondered what his boss would make of such a jumble. Bill Simon liked his private surroundings and business dealings streamlined and simplified, so he could make his personal and executive decisions as quickly and neatly as possible. Such a cool efficiency had its own appeal, but Jack sometimes preferred mucking through life's muddles—especially when he discovered the diamonds in the rough patches.

Uncut, unpolished diamonds like Sawyer's BayRock Enterprises. Buying Sawyer's company could satisfy Continental's insatiable appetite for raw materials while establishing a viable—and potentially valuable—presence north of San Francisco. And it was up to Jack to prove that viability and estimate that potential.

To streamline and simplify the muddle.

He nodded an apology for disturbing the tabby cat before opening the low picket gate and strolling up aged concrete steps to the stained-glass entry. The gingerbread tacked onto every nook and cranny made the villa look homey and fussy, giving the impression the inside was likely stuffed to its curlicued rafters with antiques and doodads.

As he stepped onto a wide wooden porch furnished with wicker and ferns, one of the lace curtains swagged across a bay window twitched discreetly and settled back into its graceful curve. Jack grinned, pleased to see his hunch had paid off. Just as he'd suspected when he'd phoned, Agatha Allen was a nosy hostess. Bed and breakfasts weren't the typical business-trip lodgings, but they often provided one benefit in addition to a comfortable place to sleep and a home-cooked meal to start the day: a built-in source of small-town gossip.

Moments after he twisted an ornate brass bell knob, a handsome woman, neat and trim and somewhere in the neighborhood of fifty, opened the heavy mahogany door.

"Agatha Allen?" he asked.

She nodded and stepped aside, waving him in. "And you must be Jack. Welcome to Villa Veneto. Oh, put that away," she said with another wave as he shifted his bag over his arm and reached into his back pocket for his wallet. "We can take care of the paperwork after you've had a chance to settle in."

She plucked a tasseled key ring from a row of hooks behind her tiny reception desk and led the way up a steep, narrow flight of stairs covered with a floral runner. "I hear you've been in the Cove practically all day already. Kate down at the Abalone waited on you at lunch, and she called to tell me you got here safe and sound, since she knew I'd be worrying. You must have caught your plane at the crack of dawn, you poor thing. I'll bet you're ready for a cup of tea. Which do you prefer—black or herbal?"

He shook his head at her back. "Neither, though I truly appreciate the offer."

"Coffee, then." Agatha tossed him a no-nonsense glance over her shoulder and nodded with a finality that let Jack know he'd be having a cup of coffee before he stepped foot out her front door again, come hell or high water.

"And something to eat," she continued. "I took the last batch of coconut macaroon cookies out of the oven not five minutes ago. I make them up to crush for my chocolate silk pie crust—and don't you go telling anyone about that secret while you're here, or I'll find out—but I can always spare a couple of cookies for a snack."

"Coconut macaroons just happen to be one of my favorites," he said.

She paused when they reached the second floor and studied him as if she were attempting to divine the truth of his statement, and he suffered through the panic of a guilty moment. He wondered what the penalty might be if she discovered he could barely tolerate coconut, in macaroons or pie crusts or anywhere else.

"And my secret?" she asked at last.

"Is safe with me," he answered with relief.

He followed her along a wide balcony and a curve in the hallway that wrapped back around the stairwell, past several tall, transomed doors punctuating rose- and lily-papered walls. Doors with exotic names calligraphied in gold paint on thickly trimmed panels: Lido, Rialto, Murano.

She stopped at the last in the line and handed him the key to the San Marco suite. "They have these in Venice, you know," she said.

"Venice?" He stared at the old-fashioned brass key in his hand, struggling to make the transition from coconut crust to canals.

"The tassels."

"Ah." He gave her a suitably impressed nod. "Nice touch."

"It's in the Italian style, you see."

"Yes," he said, although he really didn't.

"Like Versace and Armani."

"Two of my favorites," he said as he jiggled the key into the lock. He wondered what she'd think of his Armani suit and nearly regretted leaving it behind. He hadn't thought there'd be much occasion for designer labels in Carnelian Cove. "Just like coconut macaroons."

"Oh." She flipped her little wave at him again. "There's no need to lay the charm on so thick. Although I do enjoy a dose of it every once in a while, just like the next person. And especially when it comes out sounding so nice, like it does with that accent of yours. Louisiana?"

"No, ma'am. South Carolina."

"Charleston?"

He stepped into the room and spread his bag across the quilt-covered double bed. "A small place west of there. Nothing anyone's ever heard of."

Nothing—and nobody—from nowhere. That's what he'd felt like when he'd left, and that's why he'd never go back. He'd worked his way across the country and struggled for a foothold on the corporate ladder, and he'd done it on his own.

And now he was going to collect the rest of his things, and settle down for some late-afternoon coffee and cookies, and pump Agatha Allen for every shred of information he could coax out of her. He'd kick back and relax, thicken his accent a touch and see what unexpected tips it might tickle loose.

Corporate intrigue came in all shapes and sizes, even coconut macaroons.

A KELP-SCENTED, BONE-CHILLING fog thickened the darkness on Cove Street that evening when Charlie steered her truck toward A Slice of Light, the stained-glass shop owned by Addie Sutton. The jeweled tones of the samples dangling in the windows slid over her windshield as she angled into the parking space behind Tess Roussel's sporty red compact. Her two best friends in the same place at the same time—twice the sympathy, double the outrage. Fewer brownies to go around, she thought as she stuffed a pink bakery box inside a deep grocery bag and slipped out the driver's door, but the moral support would be worth it.

She needed all the support she could muster after today's potentially devastating developments.

Ignoring the Closed sign in the window, she rapped on the shop door. After a shivering wait and a second round of more insistent knocking, Tess—long-legged even without her three-inch heels—appeared in the darkened shop and sauntered over to open the door. Why the town's newest architect wanted to wrestle her way into pantyhose and thigh-hugging skirts every day was a mystery.

"Well, look what the tide washed in," said Tess. "A little red-shelled crab."

"What are you doing here?" Charlie angled past her and headed toward the long, deep counter dividing the shop's display area from Addie's work space. She paused near a table bristling with pins holding dozens of cut glass pieces in place. It was the beginning of a peacock, the body crafted in rich hues and the tail cascading in intricate detail over the jagged outline of a tree limb.

"Same as you," said Tess. "Scrounging for dinner company."

"Shouldn't you be out on some hot date with some hot dude?"

"It's Thursday. Give me another twenty-four hours." Tess closed the shop door and flipped the lock. "On the other hand, another day probably won't make a difference. I'm fresh out of hot prospects in this town. Nothing but lukewarm lately."

Charlie shot a skeptical glance at the woman with whom she'd shared every summer vacation during their school years. Tall, dark and drop-dead gorgeous, Tess had only to crook a manicured finger at any available man in Carnelian Cove to have him panting after her.

"Besides," said Tess as she brushed her short, layered hair out of her eyes, "I'm too busy being brilliant."

"And humble."

"Only when required."

Charlie followed Tess through the curtained glass door at the rear of Addie's shop and stepped into the odd apartment ranged along the building's back wall. Antique kitchen appliances lined one side of the open space, and a thrift-shop sofa and woodstove directly opposite defined the seating area. Pipes and heating ducts snaked around lighting fixtures suspended from the high ceiling. The loft effect at ground level.

She passed an old, claw-footed oak table crowded with books, rolls of paper and a fat yellow pitcher stuffed with tulips and set her package on the slanted farmhouse sink, near the wreckage of a fast-food meal. She helped herself to one of the fries heaped on wrinkled paper and waved another one toward the mess on the table. "Is that your stuff taking up all the eating space?"

"My latest sketches. Look." Tess spread one of the rolls of paper and anchored the corners with the books. "Look."

Charlie popped another fry into her mouth and wiped her hands on her jeans before studying Tess's sketch for a proposed bayside project. The opportunity to develop the property with her own design had played a major role in luring Tess from a large architectural firm in San Francisco. Charlie and Addie had been delighted when their childhood friend had hung her shingle above one of the Cove's Main Street storefronts.

"I've decided the main entrance should feature stained-glass sidelights," said Tess. "Maybe some more touches, here, and here—" she indicated "—if I can incorporate the design into the structure."

Charlie marveled again at the way Tess had managed to capture and update Carnelian Cove's architectural traditions with clean lines and decorative details. The building would add a fresh touch to the waterfront while blending in with its nineteenth-century neighbors "I hate to admit it," she said, "but you're right. You are brilliant."

"Best idea I've seen in a long time," said Addie in her low, raspy voice as she stepped around the partition screening her bedroom from the rest of her apartment. Her long blond hair fell in tangled spirals from a clip that had slipped to one side of her head. "Although I told her she should come back tomorrow morning so we can look at some glass samples in the sunlight."

Charlie traced a finger over the drawing. "All that glass looks like a lot of work."

"I could use a lot of work," Addie said. "Business has

been slow." She crossed to the sink, rummaged through the large brown bag holding Charlie's contributions to the impromptu dinner party and pulled out the pink box. "Is this from Bern's Bakery?"

"Marie-Claudette's brownies?" Tess snatched the box from Addie and ripped through the tape. "God, *yes*."

"The ones with the fudge frosting?" Addie reached around Tess and fished out a chunky pastry. "And sprinkles. Look—red ones, for Valentine's Day."

"Dibs on the blondies," said Tess.

"Don't worry. They're all yours." Addie licked dark brown frosting from the corner of her mouth. "They're disgusting."

"Just because they're not chocolate—"

"Which makes them disgusting—"

"Please." Charlie pulled her soda six-pack from the crumpled grocery sack and wrenched a can from its plastic ring. "I'm in the middle of a crisis here."

"Charlie." Addie's blue eyes darkened with worry. "What is it?"

Charlie took a long sip of her soda. "David's really done it this time."

"He convinced your mom to sell?"

"He burned down the plant?"

"He totaled his fancy new company truck?"

"He got Missy Turner pregnant?"

Charlie zeroed in on Tess. "What was that about Missy Turner?"

"Nothing. Not a thing." Tess stuffed a wedge of yellow brownie into her mouth, cutting off any chance for an explanation.

Addie pulled one of the mismatched chairs from beneath the table. "Here. Sit down." She gestured for Charlie to take the seat and gave her arm a sympathetic pat before settling into the chair beside hers. "You look beat."

"I feel beat." Charlie stared at the tulip leaves drooping over the edges of the pitcher. "Finally, totally beat."

Tess popped the top of one of the soda cans. "What happened?"

"I'm not sure yet what part David played in this," said Charlie, "but a rep from Continental showed up at the plant today."

"Continental?" Tess's eyebrows winged up in surprise. "The Continental that owns a piece of every construction firm between here and Vegas?"

Addie frowned. "What's a representative from a big company like that doing here?"

"That's exactly what I wanted to know," said Charlie. "And what—or who—put Carnelian Cove on their radar." She rubbed her temples. "He was at Earl's plant this morning, too."

"God." Tess lowered her drink to the sink's drainboard. "They're moving in."

"Looks like it."

"They want to buy BayRock?" Addie's forehead creased with worry. "But I thought Earl was going to sell it to you."

"Wait a minute." Tess folded her arms and leaned one hip against the sink. "There was this guy talking to Ramón at the self-serve pump when I stopped for gas on my lunch break. Someone I've never seen around here before.

Medium height, wavy dark blond hair. *GQ* weekend look with slightly muddy work boots. And dimples to die for. God, that smile…"

She sighed and then straightened with a guilty look in Charlie's direction. "But maybe not your guy. And probably not a genuine hot prospect."

"Liar." Charlie bit into Marie-Claudette's chewy brand of comfort. "That's him, right down to the dirty boots. And he's a hottie, all right."

"But a scary one," said Addie. "With ulterior motives."

"Definitely *not* a prospect," said Tess.

"Prospect or not, he's the enemy." Charlie took another bite of chocolate fortification. "And I'm going to take him down, dimples and all."

CHAPTER FOUR

JACK SKIPPED THE postbreakfast coffee at Agatha's early
Friday morning, likely adding another black mark to his
ledger sheet. His hostess had figured out—at some point
between her warm-from-the-oven cookie party in the
kitchen and her considerably cooler good-night greeting
on the stairway—the reason for his visit, and it was
obvious her sympathies lay with the home team.

Besides, he was eager to check out the Carnelian Cove
market for himself. Figures on spreadsheets were never as
revealing as the businesses and consumers and connections
they represented. And getting out of the office and meeting
folks had always been the best part of his job.

He'd sipped an excellent espresso in a café near the
marina, and then he'd shared a scone and an interesting
conversation with a scruffy fellow fishing from one of the
docks. He'd watched a blacksmith on Main Street shap-
ing an iron scroll for a garden gate, and he'd discussed the
difficulties of pigeon population control with a woman
scrubbing the walk in front of her knitting supply shop.

He'd needed this break in the corporate routine, he
realized as he hiked south of the marina, circling toward
Oyster Lane. Needed to clear his mind and reorganize

his priorities. Needed to concentrate on one of the most important reasons for this trip: gathering more ammunition for the skirmishes brewing in the San Francisco office.

Bill, his boss, hadn't yet answered his morning call—most likely preoccupied with pinning down the source of the latest corporate rumors and more cautious than usual about the dicey projects Jack had made his specialty. Projects like this foray north to Carnelian Cove. Noah Fuller, Jack's perennial rival and general pain in the butt, was eager to take advantage of the situation, looking to sink this deal—and Jack with it. And Jack's assistant was pressuring him to cut his trip short and fly back south to defend his office turf from another of Noah's coup attempts.

Calls, coups, pressure. Jack kicked at a pebble wedged in a sidewalk crack, wishing he could get rid of his problems as easily. He liked his job, and he enjoyed living in San Francisco. But there were parts of any job he'd ever had, and aspects of any location he'd ever lived in, that had shredded his patience and dampened his spirit and made him consider moving on.

He'd been on the move for over a dozen of his thirty-two years, heading west until he'd reached the ocean at the other side of the continent. And no matter where he headed now, he'd run up against the same types of shifting, fluid obstacles, the same office politics and the same corporate insecurities. Best to hunker down and pull off a coup of his own here in Carnelian Cove, to blast Noah out of his path and earn another recommendation for a promotion from his grateful boss. He was too young to feel so tired and worn, particularly on such a promising day in a town full of possibilities.

He rounded a corner and discovered the source of the construction-related clatter he'd heard across the water. Up ahead, a concrete pump operator wound thick black hoses over his screen trailer, and another driver washed out a Keene mixer angled near the muddy gash of a job site. Curious about the project, Jack ambled toward the crew laboring over a freshly poured slab.

One of the finishers stretched his float in practiced swoops across the glossy, wet surface of a new drive, while another knelt to scrape deep joints in the mix with a trowel. Though finishing concrete had never been one of his favorite chores, Jack itched to pick up one of the tools and get his hands dirty. Moments like this made him miss the hands-on satisfaction of the construction business and yearn for more opportunities to get out of the office.

Behind the crew, a taller-than-average man with wavy black hair pitched a cell phone into the cab of a black pickup truck. "Can I help you?" he asked.

"Just watching, if that's okay." Jack extended his hand. "Jack Maguire."

The dark-haired man wiped his hand on his jeans before shaking Jack's. "Quinn. You the man from Continental?"

"Word gets around," said Jack with a grin.

Quinn's mouth tightened in a thin line that might have passed for a smile if his level stare had warmed a degree or two. But it didn't. "Is Continental putting in a bid on Sawyer's outfit?" he asked.

"Not sure." Jack studied the finishing work. "Depends on the market around here. The supply."

"The customers."

"That, too."

Jack already knew Quinn was considered one of the best contractors in the area. He had a steady crew, did the job well and on time and paid his bills promptly. Agatha had offered a few more details with her macaroons: in spite of his professional reputation for quality work, Quinn's personal reputation—as a recovering alcoholic with a troublesome past—kept him scrambling more than most for opportunities to keep his crew employed and his redemption on track.

"In my experience," said Jack with a glance at the Keene mixer, "customers tend to be loyal to one supplier."

"Unless there's enough incentive to switch." Quinn raised one shoulder in a casual shrug. "Might be a one-time deal, though. Loyalty and all."

Jack matched Quinn's shrug with one of his own. "You get what you pay for."

Quinn gave him another long, level stare and then nodded and moved off to check on his crew. Loyalty was an admirable virtue, and Jack understood better than most how it greased the gears of small-town economics, but the home-team advantage wouldn't last long if it came at a premium price.

He glanced up to watch gulls swoop overhead, searching for scraps. Scavengers had a purpose and a place in life, too. But all in all, he mused as he shoved his hands back into his pockets and started the trek toward the Villa Veneto, he'd rather be a hawk than a gull.

CHARLIE COASTED TO THE curb in front of her mother's house an hour after dark on Friday night. She pulled the key from the ignition and slumped in her seat, waiting for hunger to override the temptation to skip another rerun of her real-life family feud.

Dad had been fond of saying the reason his daughter and his wife couldn't understand each other better was because they were two peas in a pod. When she was young, Charlie had spent a lot of time wondering what alien legume life form Dad had had in mind when he'd made that crack.

She was in no mood to face the coming scene with her mother. The day had been a trial, starting before dawn with a couple of big pours and continuing with David's stubborn resistance to engage in a meaningful discussion about BayRock. She'd spent a tense lunch hour reminding Earl about all the reasons he'd agreed to sell BayRock to the Keenes—and reassuring him he'd have a business left to sell once she'd sent the visitor from Continental packing.

Now all she had to do was figure out a way to do it. She'd imagined every worst-case scenario and best-case possibility, plotted her way through every twist and turn, and all she had to show for the long day of physical labor and mental efforts were a headache and a queasy stomach.

She was still sitting there a quarter of an hour later, staring at the mellow light glowing through her mother's ruffly gingham curtains hanging from slightly sagging café rods. Charlie had banned ruffles and gingham from her house on the other side of town, along with Jell-O, doilies, Barry Manilow or anything pink. She was also opposed, on nearly religious principles, to anything that could be done to a woman in a beauty parlor.

It wasn't just a matter of style; her differences with her mother went deeper than that. While Charlie had always struggled for independence, Maudie Keene had cultivated clinging as a survival tactic. She'd had more than thirty years to practice the technique on her husband.

And now, Charlie thought as she watched her brother's overdeveloped, overpriced truck muscle its way into their mother's driveway, Maudie was directing the full force of her neediness at her son. In spite of Charlie's frustrations with her brother, she didn't envy him the burden of their mother's insecurities.

She climbed out of her truck. "David. Wait up."

He turned at the sound of her voice and shifted a paper bag to one hip. "What are you doing here?"

"Same as you. Getting a free meal."

"Nothing's free in this house," said David.

She bit back her reply. No point in starting an argument before they sat down together at the table. He had his own reasons for his resentment. "Well," she said, "tonight we're getting dinner in trade. What's in the bag?"

"Beer. She never has any in the house since Dad died. And ice cream. She asked me to pick some up, 'cause she made apple cobbler."

"Yeah?"

"Yeah."

They stood for a moment, awkward with sharing an appreciation for their mother's cobbler in the midst of everything dividing them. "Go ahead and knock," he said. "My hands are full."

Maudie opened the door, her large brown eyes shadowed with a habitual anxious expression. The silver threads winding through her hair—a faded version of David's rich, dark red—glinted in the porch light. "Come in, come in. Is that the ice cream? Better get it in the freezer."

David brushed past them both, heading for the back of the house. Maudie rubbed her hands on her apron and stared after him. "I made cobbler."

"So I heard." Charlie shrugged out of her coat and tossed it over one of the hooks on the coat rack. "Sounds great, Mom."

"Pot roast, too. With extra gravy. Just the way you like it."

"And potato chunks? The crispy ones?"

"Of course."

"Mmm." Charlie took a deep breath and let it out on a long sigh, trying to ease away some of the tension with it. "Makes my mouth water just thinking about it."

Maudie beamed at the compliment and toyed with the edge of her apron. "I don't mind the extra trouble. It's nice to have some company at a meal for a change."

An appetizer of guilt served before the first course. It was going to be a long evening.

"Mom," David called from the kitchen. "How come the table's set for four?"

"I forgot to mention." Maudie blushed and lifted a fluttering hand to smooth her hair. "Ben's joining us."

Ben Chandler. It was difficult to imagine her mother

having romantic feelings for someone else. Charlie pasted on a smile. "It'll be good to see him again."

Maudie smiled. "I'd better see to the gravy." She turned and walked down the hall, her stylish pumps clicking over the wood floor. She was a trim woman who looked younger than her age, an energetic woman who filled her mornings with volunteer activities and lunched with friends in the afternoon. Which left the evenings…

Her mother. And Ben Chandler.

Charlie took a deep breath and stepped into the front room. She wasn't sure she approved of her mother's flushed cheeks or the reason for the pearl earrings and the dressy green sweater beneath the apron, but she approved of Ben. He'd maintained his dignity and reputation while so many members of the wealthy and influential Chandler clan had ruined their lives with drink and disastrous choices.

And he'd helped keep David in check. As Maudie's financial adviser, Ben had cautioned against making any decisions about selling Keene Concrete until all the ramifications could be considered. And it hadn't been difficult for Charlie to provide enough complications to keep things tied up for months.

But Ben hadn't yet been able to reassure Maudie that her investments of the insurance funds or her bonuses from the family company would keep pace with her expenses. Maudie seemed obsessed with running her own figures and making her own calculations and projections, so much so that Charlie had wondered if Ben would quit in frustration. Instead, he'd listen quietly, nodding and smiling, and then he'd go over the figures with her one more time. He seemed to have an endless supply of patience where her mother was concerned.

Charlie wandered into the front room to stare at the family photos lined up like soldiers on the brick mantel. There was Dad, standing on the riverbank with a long fish dangling from the line and a wide grin on his face. There he was again, with another smile for the six-year-old daughter on his lap as he guided her hand toward the controls of an old loader. And there was her favorite, the shot of her parents at a holiday costume party, dressed as pirates.

David stepped behind her. "They always looked so happy."

"Don't you think they were?"

"No couple is happy all the time."

She turned to face him. "Maybe not, but at least they did their best to hide most of the bad times from us."

"Sheltered us, you mean."

"What's wrong with that? What's wrong with that kind of security?"

"Security." David shook his head. "Is that why you're trying so hard to hold everything in place?"

"You still don't get it, do you?" She took a deep breath and tried, for the hundredth time, to get through to him. "Dad handed us something lots of people never have in their lifetime. The opportunity to work for ourselves. The chance to build something that belongs to *us*."

"We don't have that chance, Charlie. It's already built. He did it." David glanced behind her to the row of photos. "And as long as we keep Keene Concrete, we'll keep working for him."

A knock on the door summoned their mother from the kitchen. "That must be Ben," she said as she passed through the front room. "Charlie, would you mind getting the rolls from the oven to the table? There's a basket for them near the sink."

David followed Charlie into the kitchen. "What's up with Mom and Ben?"

"I think they're seeing each other."

"Isn't that unethical?" David scowled. "He shouldn't be discussing money matters with her if he's trying to get her into bed."

"Please." Charlie squeezed her eyes shut. "I don't want to think about it."

"Face it, Charlie. She's going to hook up with someone as fast as she can. Mom can't handle being alone."

"She's been doing okay so far." Charlie dumped the rolls into the basket. Her mother probably would have arranged them in some more attractive fashion, but Charlie figured they'd get eaten no matter how they looked. "I just hope she doesn't rush into something she'll regret."

"I don't like him."

"Who, Ben?"

David's eyes narrowed. "I don't trust him."

"I do."

"That's because he always takes your side."

"Maybe that's because I'm always right."

She caught him by the arm before he could turn and stalk from the room. "We need to talk—all of us. About the timing of the visit from the Continental rep. About what might happen if Earl sells to someone other than Keene, and how we're going to handle it."

"What's the point of talking? Your mind's already made up, just like always."

"And you're not thinking things through." She closed her eyes and scrambled for patience. "I'm sorry. I don't want to fight. I need your help with this, David."

"You don't need anyone. That's the problem."

Their mother walked into the kitchen with a clutch of daffodils. "Aren't these pretty? Ben brought them for the table."

"I'm glad he's here," said Charlie. "We need to talk."

"Not business," said Maudie with a sigh. "Not tonight."

"Maybe it's for the best, Maudie." Ben stood in the doorway, steady and solemn, tall and broad shouldered. His silver-gray suit seemed to match his silver hair, and he looked every inch the successful owner of a respected accounting firm. "I understand there's something we all need to discuss. Isn't that right, Charlie?"

She nodded slowly, dreading the dinner conversation to come. "Yes," she said. "I think a discussion would be good." She glanced at David. "Arriving at an agreement would be even better."

CHAPTER FIVE

THE FRIDAY NIGHT CROWD at The Shantyman was an interesting mix of baby-faced university students and hard-edged locals. The younger crowd formed a background of color and motion, shooting billiard balls into side pockets or shuffling around the stingy dance floor while the older, monochromatic drinkers hunched over the tiny tables aligned like a string of beads against a dark plank wall. The murmur of conversation rose and fell like ocean swells, competing with the jukebox rock pumping from the corner.

Jack searched for a neutral zone between the two groups—each ignoring the other with mutual tolerance—and found a spot at the bar directly beneath a television tuned to a college basketball game. He ordered a microbrew from the distillery down the road and settled in to pass the evening drinking up the community buzz.

"Well, if it isn't the man from the city."

The woman from the gas pump, the leggy brunette with the boy's haircut and the come-hither smile, slid onto the next stool. "Checking out the local scene?" she asked.

He raised his glass in acknowledgment. "How'd you know I was from San Francisco?"

"News spreads." The smile she gave him this time didn't

quite reach her dark eyes. "But with an accent like that, you didn't start out from there."

He waited while she ordered a diet cola. "Why don't you ask me a question you don't already know the answer to. Might make for a more interesting conversation."

"You have a point. Especially since I'm here to ask you lots of questions."

He eased back and gestured with the bottle. "Shoot."

"Tempting," she said, "but I think I'll wait until I've got some answers."

He sipped his beer and studied her cool, assessing expression. "Answer a question for me."

"All right," she said after a brief pause. "Seems fair."

"Married?"

"Loyal."

He shrugged and took another sip of his beer. "Good as, then."

"That's right." She leaned an elbow on the bar. "And if you understand that, then you'll understand why I'm not going to like you very much."

"Now, that's a pure waste of the home-team advantage," he said with a smile to prove his point, "'cause I'm a fairly likable guy."

"Hmm." She took her soda from the barkeep and jabbed the little red straw between the ice cubes. "I'm beginning to see that. Which will make this even more entertaining."

"Is that him?" A curvy blonde with party-streamer hair, china-doll eyes and a glass of white wine took a seat next to the woman with the attitude. "Looks like he fits the description."

"That's him, all right."

"Jackson Maguire," he said, extending his hand toward the newcomer with the husky voice. "Folks call me Jack."

She gave his hand a quick shake. "Addie Sutton."

He stared at Addie's neighbor and waited as she let him dangle for a moment. "Tess Roussel," she said at last as she slid her hand into his.

"Friends of Charlie Keene's?"

"Sounds like a question you already know the answer to." Tess picked up her straw and returned to abusing the ice in her drink. "You catch on quick, city boy."

"Not too hard to do," he said, "when she's standing at the door staring daggers at the two of you."

CHARLIE YANKED AT THE HEM of her flannel shirt and made her way to the bar where her traitorous friends perched, cozying up to the competition. Bad enough she had to deal with Call-Me-Jack Maguire on the job and worry about what he was up to on an overtime basis. She deeply resented the fact that he was invading her downtime, too.

Particularly when he looked so ridiculously good doing it. Those long, lean legs of his folded around that bar stool as if they'd been made just for that purpose, and his muscled shoulders stretched his shirt across a wide back. His wavy hair glinted like old gold coins in the mellow bar light and brushed over the edges of his collar.

"Evenin', Charlie," he said with one of his crinkly, craggy smiles. "What can I get for you?"

"Are you an employee of this establishment?"

"Nope."

"Then it's not your job to get my drink."

"That's right." He stretched the words like a taffy pull with that slow, sly drawl of his. "It's my pleasure."

"Did you buy their drinks, too?" She jerked her thumb at Tess's cola and Addie's wine.

"We didn't give him a chance," said Addie.

Tess shrugged. "He didn't offer."

Jack sipped his brew and lowered the mug to the counter. "A mistake I won't be making a second time, ladies."

"That's all right," said Tess. "There are hundreds of other mistakes you can make."

"Thousands," said Addie.

"He won't be staying that long." Charlie dragged over a nearby stool and wedged it between her so-called friends, avoiding the vacant seat beside Jack. "I'm surprised you're still here. It can be slow in the Cove on weekends. Not as many opportunities to cause trouble as there are in the city."

"I thought I'd stick around and enjoy the scenery like the rest of the tourists."

"You're not a tourist," said Charlie. "And it's not tourist season."

"You could take a drive up the bluff road, past Chandler House," Addie told him. "It's got some nice views."

Tess gave her a disapproving glance. "Yeah, and some tricky curves," she added. "Gotta watch out for those sheer drops at the shoulder of the road. Or…not."

"He doesn't have time for leisurely drives," said Charlie. "He's leaving in a few days. Next week. Monday, probably."

"Now, I don't know about that." Jack grabbed a bowl of pretzels and shoved them toward Charlie. "I've always been one of those overachieving types. Might want to stick around a bit longer than expected, just to prove the point."

"So…you're not leaving on Monday?" asked Addie.

"Guess not," said Tess. "Sounds like he's going to hang around and make as many of those mistakes as possible." She chose one of the pretzels and glanced at Jack. "Try Pale Paisley, while you're at it."

He raised an eyebrow. "Paisley?"

"Charlie's favorite," said Addie, trying to be helpful, as usual. "It's local."

He motioned for the bartender, and Charlie tugged Tess close enough to whisper in her ear. "What are you doing?"

"Having some fun at your expense." Tess shrugged. "It's a hell of a lot cheaper than having it at my own."

"Lighten up, Charlie," said Addie as she helped herself to a pretzel. "Tess was giving him a pretty rough time before you got here."

"My pleasure," said Tess. "You know, he's even cuter up close. We could toy with him awhile before we bring out the thumbscrews."

"He's all yours." Charlie scowled at the frosted mug and the bottle of beer the bartender placed in front of her. "Thank you."

"What was that, darlin'?" asked Jack.

Charlie shot him a lethal look. "Thank you."

"You're welcome."

He slid from his stool and extended a hand to Addie. "This song's one of my favorites. Come and dance a memory with me, pretty lady."

"What a surprisingly sweet invitation." Addie placed her hand in his. "How can I resist?"

Charlie nearly spilled her beer. *"Addie."*

"Well, how can I?" asked Addie with one of her trade-mark wide-eyed, innocent looks.

Jack led her to the center of the tiny dance floor, slipped an arm around her waist and stepped into the rhythm as if they were old friends who'd done this kind of thing a dozen times. Or old lovers, the way he pulled Addie close and spread his fingers across her back. Charlie scowled at them both and turned to pour more beer into her glass.

"That man has some seriously smooth moves," said Tess. "Wouldn't mind finding out how effective they are."

Charlie set the bottle down with a *clunk*. "You, too?"

"Hey." Tess swirled her straw through her soda. "Single guy. Single gal. Friday night out. Perfect cover for some serious espionage. You ought to take advantage of the situation yourself."

"I don't need to spy on the competition. And he happens to be a single guy from the big city who's threatening to put one of your best friends out of business."

"Did he actually say that?"

"He didn't have to."

Tess sipped her drink. "Don't you think you're being a touch overdramatic here?"

"Guess you'd be the judge of that," Charlie muttered.

"I heard that."

Charlie glared at Jack as he whispered something in Addie's ear. Addie tossed her head back with a laugh, and her long hair swung loose as he spun her in a turn.

Tess set her drink on the counter and leaned in close. "The thing is, I don't understand why Continental's sniffing around here at all. This isn't exactly what I'd call a booming market."

Charlie nodded. "That's what I intend to find out."

Addie reclaimed her stool, and Charlie turned to find Jack grinning at Tess.

"Your turn, Slim," he said. "Come and help me make mistake number two."

"Number three." Tess cast a pointed glance at Charlie, wiggled off her stool and smoothed a hand over her dress.

Jack's eyes followed every move. "A guy's got to appreciate a female who knows the score," he said with a wicked grin.

Charlie rolled her eyes toward the smoke-stained ceiling as Jack led Tess out to the dance floor. Beside her, Addie leaned her chin on her hand with a long, wistful sigh.

"Did you two have fun?" asked Charlie.

"He's a very good dancer."

"Tess said he had some smooth moves." Charlie shredded the edge of her napkin. "Did he put one on you?"

Addie straightened and lifted her chin. "What makes you think I'd let him?"

"I don't."

"I'm not so sure about that." Addie twisted the stem of her glass, looking wounded and making Charlie want to crawl over the beer-tacky floor and beg for forgiveness. "You're making too much of every little thing tonight," said Addie. "Makes me wonder why."

"Must be the rotten mood I'm in." Charlie bit into a

pretzel. "I get that way when my friends chum up to the guy who's out to destroy my family business."

"It's not chummy," said Addie, "it's polite. And social. Tess will explain the difference when she finishes dancing—which happens to be another acceptable form of social activity. Besides, we were only trying to help."

She closed her hand over Charlie's. "I'm sorry you're upset. We thought an evening out would cheer you up."

"I know." Charlie stared into her mug. "You're usually so good at it, too. I should be more grateful."

"But then you wouldn't be you." Addie gave her fingers a pat. "Don't worry. I have a feeling everything will turn out for the best."

"You always feel that way." Good old Addie—always looking on the bright side. Charlie managed to dredge up her first genuine smile of the evening—a smile that quickly dimmed when she glanced over her shoulder to see Jack standing behind her, cocky and handsome and far too sure of himself. Far too tempting.

"Where's Tess?" she asked.

"Fanning herself in the lady's fanning room." He plucked at his shirt. "I'd say we worked up some heat on the dance floor, but you might call the vice squad and have me thrown in jail."

"We don't have anything as fancy as a vice squad around here." She swiveled on her seat to face him. "But for a special visitor like you, we could arrange a night in the stocks on Main Street."

The other side of his mouth lifted in one of his slow smiles, the kind that lit each corner of his face before settling and sparkling in his eyes. Right on cue, her stomach knotted up, threatening to do something nasty to all that beer she'd poured down there.

"Okay, Charlie," he said. "Your turn."

"Oops, look at that." She raised an empty hand. "No dance ticket. Guess I lost my place in line."

"No problem." Jack took her hand, tipping her off balance and into his arms.

"Hey." She made a weak attempt to push him away and an even weaker attempt to ignore the feel of hard muscle and the scent of warm male. "I didn't say yes."

"And I didn't hear you say no." He closed his fingers around hers in a gentle but steely grip and led her toward the dance floor. "Come on, Charlie. Make things easy for once."

"I'm better at making them difficult."

"A rare and useful talent, and one that deserves a great deal of respect." He tugged her up against him, and the shock of the contact with his solid body knocked the wind out of her snappy comeback. "But right now," he said, "I'd just like to sway back and forth while we get to know each other better."

While we get to know each other better. Tess had been right about his moves. Jack Maguire had a way of placing his hands and pressing his fingertips just so, a way of starting something with his steps and following through with his body that was just right. A way of making a woman feel all the things his voice promised—dreamy and tingly and wicked—all at once. Against her will, Charlie softened against him, one sticky degree at a time, while Diana Krall crooned some number about being a lucky so-and-so.

Oh, my, this was nice—and Diana on the jukebox couldn't possibly be feeling what Charlie was feeling at the moment. What she shouldn't be feeling, although it was very nice indeed. There were too many interested bystanders in this public place, too many people who knew her history with men. And the thought of adding another loss to her scorecard was enough to siphon all the pleasure out of the experience.

"I don't want to get to know you better," she said, though she'd caught a glimpse of dark blond hair peeking from beneath his open shirt collar and was imagining the way it might spread across his wide chest. "And I don't dance."

"You don't have to dance. All you have to do is take a step or two and follow my lead." He lowered his head until his mouth was inches from hers and his warm breath brushed her face. "Could be the beginning of a beautiful and mutually beneficial relationship."

CHAPTER SIX

CHARLIE'S BACK TENSED AGAIN, and Jack eased away a fraction of an inch. She was right about one thing, he decided as he steered her stiff and stubborn body around the miserly square of parquet floor—she couldn't dance. No sense of rhythm that he could discern, and no feel for the subtle nudges or the interesting directions a conversation could take when a woman's body—stubborn or otherwise—pressed up against a man's. He'd bet she wouldn't recognize a double entendre if one bit her on that miniature butt of hers.

The butt he was surprisingly tempted to measure with his hands.

"I don't want to have a relationship with you," she said, picking up her snarl where she'd left off. "Beneficial or not."

"I've heard any number of things this evening you don't want." He guided her through a clumsy twirl, trying to derail the single thought traveling along that one-track mind of hers. "Isn't there anything you *do* want?"

"I want you to go back where you came from."

"And so I shall, at some point."

He seized another opportunity to simply look at her

again, since she'd obliged him by tipping her chin up toward his. If a fellow could get past the mulish expression, her features were kind of pleasing, in an unexpected way. Her eyes were too large for her angular face, her nose too short, her chin too square. The freckles were a bonus, adding a touch of whimsy. The combination worked somehow—and the personality animating it added a certain bristly allure to the mix.

"In the meantime," he said, "for the next few minutes, why don't you just relax and enjoy the music."

"I don't want—"

He tightened his hold on her waist, pulling her closer. "Something told me I was about to hear those words again."

She stumbled and then caught up with his easy, steady steps. Her soft, curly hair tickled his chin, and he breathed in her clean scent. Nothing floral or herbal, no tropical fruits or exotic musks for Charlie Keene. More like the smell of the freshly washed linens flapping on the line strung across his mama's back porch on a summer afternoon.

She shifted to one side, and her slender thigh grazed the outside of his knee. A familiar heavy, warm sensation began to pulse through his system, and he realized he was enjoying this dance too much—considering whom he was enjoying it with.

He set some distance between them. "You know," he said, "acting in such a predictable manner might tip your hand in a tricky negotiation."

She glared at him. "Are you giving me business advice now?"

"You don't need much, from what I've seen. And heard."

The song came to an end, but she stayed where she was, one hand on his shoulder and the other clasped in his. "Just what have you heard?" she asked.

"Now, Charlie, you don't expect me to simply hand over the results of all my weeks of diligent research, do you?"

"Research?" Her hand slid off his shoulder as her frown deepened. "On me?"

"I don't believe in heading into a job without checking out the lay of the land." Or the players in it.

Charlie's reactions to his touch tonight had proved that Agatha's casual breakfast gossip that morning had been correct. The woman standing before him, her small hand resting soft and warm in his, had never outgrown her schoolgirl reputation as a tomboy, and as a result had chalked up a pitiful dating history. He doubted she'd had more than a handful of meaningful encounters with a man outside the mechanics shop. She certainly didn't appear to know how to take the measure of a man's interest and use it to her advantage.

Not that he'd ever allow her to use his interest in such a manner.

She pulled herself up so straight he could have sworn she'd swallowed a length of rebar. "I wouldn't use the word *lay* in a tricky business negotiation, if I were you."

He'd just lost his personal bet about entendres, double or nothing. "My apologies, ma'am."

"I'm not a ma'am."

"Sorry, but it appears so, particularly from where I'm standing."

She tugged her hand free. "Which is entirely too close."

She was right about that, because he suddenly realized how much closer he wanted to get. He tested them both by shifting in her direction. She flinched but held her ground, and he managed to stop himself from taking her into his arms when the next bluesy tune throbbed from the machine beside them.

"You know something, Charlie Keene?" He rewarded himself with another teasing touch, tucking a flyaway curl behind her ear. "You're one of the most challenging partners I've ever had the pleasure of dancing with."

She batted his hand away when it lingered too long near her cheek. "You won't think it's a pleasure for long."

"My, that nearly sounded like a threat."

"Good." She shook her head to free the trapped curl. "For a while back there at the bar, I thought there might be something wrong with your hearing."

"God almighty." He gave her a wide, delighted smile. "You are one hell of a contrary woman."

"Be still, my heart." She clapped a hand over her double-A chest. "Do you treat all your dance partners to conversations like this?"

"Only the challenging and contrary ones."

The crowd watching the television howled with derision at something on the screen. Charlie stepped back and turned away, starting a slow-motion escape. "You won't win, you know." The smug expression she flashed over her shoulder issued a challenge all its own. "I won't let you."

"You can't stop me."

"We'll see about that."

He followed her toward the bar. "Does it mean that much to you?"

She spun to face him. "It means *everything* to me. This is personal, Jack, not business. Your research must have told you that."

Yes, it had. Charlie's entire life was wrapped up tight in her family's company. Any action he took here in Carnelian Cove had the potential to devastate her. But if he was going to do his job—and do it as well as he needed to in order to achieve his own goals—he had to ignore the personal aspects of this deal and concentrate on the business angles.

"My research didn't tell me how much I'd enjoy dancing with you, Charlie." He flicked a finger down her short, freckled nose, surprised by his unexpected response to her. "Or how much I'd like to do this again sometime. Sometime very soon."

Her expression clouded with confusion and something that looked suspiciously like vulnerability. Something that tugged at his gut and made him want to make all her troubles disappear. He wasn't sure he liked this Charlie Keene—the stiff and snotty version was a much easier woman to deal with.

Whatever had happened to shake her composure, she wrestled it under control and raised her chin. "Get over it, Maguire."

She turned on her boot heel and swaggered away, heading toward her friends. He thought about going after her, about saying good-night to Tess and Addie and getting in the last word or two, but the game was over for the night. Score tied, zero-to-zero.

Damn. He hated when that happened.

RESEARCH.

Charlie moved the cursor over the next selection on her monitor on Saturday afternoon and pressed the mouse. Two could play this game, and she intended to win the next round. *All* the rounds.

She'd already put in calls to a couple of northern California aggregate producers her father had met at trade shows. They knew of Jack Maguire, had heard from others who'd dealt with him. The general consensus was that Jack was a great guy to have a drink with, someone who had some interesting stories to tell. A man who'd worked plenty of jobs in plenty of places before working his way up through the ranks at Continental, a man who knew what he was talking about and never promised more than he could deliver. A guy with a sharp wit and a sharper mind.

A gust of wind rattled her office window, and she glanced at the sky. The remains of the morning clouds hung in tatters, shredded by a north wind delivering a few days of clearer skies and dropping temperatures. She longed to be home, soaking in the hot spray of her shower, rinsing away the powdery film coating her clothes and hair since dawn, when she'd climbed up inside the batch plant to unclog the cement bin. She wanted to throw a stick for her dog, Hardy, or take him to the beach for a run. But someone had to answer the phones and load the trucks for the sparse weekend deliveries. Gus had the day off, and

David had chosen not to respond to the messages she'd left. Her turn to take the Saturday shift. Again.

She clicked back to her original search page and scanned the list. *Acquisitions specialist Jackson Maguire was quoted...Maguire, a market expert...Continental Construction's quarterly earnings...market share...considering the offer from Moore...buyout rumors spreading...*

"A buyout," she muttered as she chose one link and then another, following the trail. "Well, well, well. Now isn't this interesting."

She hunched forward, and her lips spread in a grim smile as she read a brief headline above a financial news column. "'Continental makes an attractive target for buyout specialists.' Hmm."

Click. Back to the search box to add a new key word. *Click.* "'Moore Enterprises poised to make a formal offer for Continental.'"

She noted the entry date and leaned back in her chair, staring at another tiny headline on the monitor. "Looks like BayRock isn't the only 'hot property in play.'"

Lenny, one of Keene's drivers, grabbed the jamb and leaned into her office. "If that's the last of it, I'm taking off."

"Yeah, that's it. Thanks, Lenny."

She stood and followed him down the hall to the dispatcher's desk, where they checked the orders and start times for Monday. "How's Trina doing?" she asked.

"Getting huge." Lenny tipped back his gimme cap and scratched his scalp. "Baby's due any time now."

"Maybe you won't be here on Monday."

His narrow face lit up with a tobacco-stained grin. "Maybe not."

"Say hey to Trina for me. And do me a favor and lock the gate on your way out, will you?"

"Will do, boss." He waved as he headed out the door. "See you Monday."

Lenny needed this job, needed to keep his health insurance policy for Trina and the baby. He'd been working every day possible during the winter slow season, scrounging for scrap hours from other drivers with higher seniority, cheerfully filling in on weekends, adding to his savings. The responsibility for Lenny and her other employees weighed on Charlie like a ten-yarder with a full load.

She closed the door behind him, headed back to her office and slipped into her chair. As she read more articles, her concept of the threat from Continental fractured into a different set of puzzle pieces, and she slowly began to assemble some new strategies to deal with the challenges.

Construction giant Continental was scrambling for its own footing in a shifting market, faced with a buyout offer from an even bigger company, an offer its board of directors might consider too generous to ignore. Jackson Maguire might soon be out of a job—or called off the one he was involved in at the moment.

Charlie shoved out of her chair to pace her office. Jack was a sharp guy—everyone said so. He had to know about the potential buyout of Continental. So why in the world was he up here on such an unlikely shopping trip at a time like this?

She slipped her hands into her back pockets and stared out her window. "What are you up to, Maguire?"

Maybe he was simply on a routine fishing expedition to see what tasty guppy he might hook for his company—whichever company that turned out to be. Maybe he was maneuvering to make a good impression on a potential new boss, or trying to give his current one another bargaining chip. Maybe she didn't have to worry as much about his presence here as she'd thought she did.

Maybe all she had to do was hold him off, to stall his progress here until someone put in a successful bid for Continental. Chances were this small corner of the world would quickly be forgotten in the resulting corporate shuffle.

For the immediate future, anyway.

And in the meantime, she'd have a chance to shore up her defenses and prepare for the next assault—if one was headed her way. Maybe she could discourage another shopping expedition by increasing the size of her company, snapping up the lion's share of the local market and gaining control of most of the local rock supply. Without a source of material, no one would ever be able to compete. And no one would ever be able to force her to sell.

Buying BayRock wasn't merely a business move that made sense for Keene Concrete. It might be essential for its survival.

She had to act now, before Maguire had a chance to buy a few drinks for Earl, to tell him some interesting stories and make a bunch of promises she'd have to outdo. She crossed to her desk, picked up her phone and punched in the number for Earl's plant. It was edging past lunchtime, but maybe Earl was taking advantage of the break in the weather to get some repair work done. From what she'd seen of his gravel plant, he could put the winter slowdown to good use.

"Hi, Ronnie," she said when BayRock's dispatcher answered. "Is Earl there?"

"He came in real early this morning, and then he took off with that guy from the Bay Area."

"Maguire?"

"That's the one." The radio in Earl's office crackled to life, and Ronnie told one of his drivers to head back to the plant. "He showed up a few minutes after Earl, and the two of them took off in Maguire's car. Sounded like they were going fishing."

"Fishing?"

"Yeah. Maguire chartered a boat and—"

Ronnie broke off to deal with another radio call, and Charlie chewed a nail. *Fishing.* Earl had always wanted to do some ocean fishing. He talked about it off and on, but he was too cheap to part with the fee for a day's charter. Had he mentioned it to Maguire? Or had Maguire—

Research.

That had to be it. The timing and choice of this outing couldn't be a coincidence. Maguire seemed to have more connections, resources and informers than the FBI, the CIA and the local ladies auxiliary put together.

She wouldn't put it past him to be charming the ladies on his lunch hour.

And now he was out there somewhere on a boat with Earl, one-on-one, drinking beer and swapping stories, doing business the manly way—bonding over slimy, smelly animals and cutting Keene Concrete out of the picture.

She winced and stared at her finger. She'd drawn blood.

"Tell Earl I called," she said when Ronnie came back on the line. "If he gets a chance, he can reach me at home tonight."

She dropped the receiver and stood in the quiet, empty office as the wind drove a scrap of cloud overhead and darkened the gray landscape beyond the windows. Doubts and insecurities swirled inside her, clawing at her weak spots before settling like lead in her gut. Mitch's little girl, trying to fill her father's boots. David's bossy sister, playing at a man's business. Maudie's dateless daughter, never keeping a man's interest with that habit of wearing the pants in a relationship.

And she'd been so desperate to prove she could handle things, focused on following her father's example while making her own mark in the local construction industry. So intent on keeping Jack in his place—and business between them—that she'd nearly missed the big picture.

She hadn't played it smart at The Shantyman the night before. What harm was there, after all, in a drink and a dance shared by a single man and a single woman? She'd allowed her personal reaction to the handsome, charming Continental rep to distract her from her primary goal: buying BayRock.

It was time to deal with things in a calm, rational manner. Time to face and accept the personal complications and use them to her advantage. After all, drinking and dancing could be rather pleasant stalling methods.

The thought of facing more reactions and distractions, of inviting Jack Maguire to complicate her goals sent a long, liquid shiver through her. She'd have to figure out how to deal with that, too.

CHAPTER SEVEN

TWO HOURS LATER, after calling Ben Chandler to discuss her research results, Charlie double-checked the dispatching assignments for Monday morning and shut down the plant. Her quick stop at the neighborhood convenience store for some milk and eggs lengthened inconveniently when she got trapped in a chat with a former elementary school teacher, and another hour had passed before Charlie turned down a narrow, potholed road in Driftwood, the residential area south of town where she lived.

Tomorrow, she promised herself as she turned into her gravel drive and switched off the ignition, she'd trim the grass in her front yard. After she'd moved the rest of that woodpile to the shed. And she should probably get the mower blades sharpened, she thought as she pulled the groceries into her lap. Maybe she'd buy some of those bright, flat flowers with the funny-looking leaves—primroses, she thought they were called—at the nursery while she was waiting for the mower to be serviced, and then she'd fill that old barrel with some fresh dirt and...

Fat chance. She'd probably sleep until noon and head back to her office after a late breakfast to check the company books.

She slid out of her truck, itchy with cement and rubbery with exhaustion, and then she smiled at the one male in her life who would never care how she looked or what she wore or whether her house was as messy as her office. "Hey there, Hardy," she said as she shifted the groceries to one hip and reached for one of the sticks dotting her yard. "Did you have a good day? Did you miss me? Did you?"

The black Labrador retriever leaped and squirmed behind the crooked wire fence, yelping his welcome-home greeting in reply. She flipped the catch and braced for the usual attack. "Down, boy," she ordered as the dog bounded out, spun around and rammed her from the side. "Get down. *Down.*"

She tossed the stick toward the redwoods crowding the fence line, and the young dog raced after it. Arching to stretch her back, she stared at the snug, Craftsman-era bungalow she'd financed with her hard-earned savings and waited for the satisfaction of ownership to lift her spirits, but the usual sense of accomplishment was dulled by the burdens of upkeep and anxiety about the future.

She tossed Hardy's stick again and trudged up the sagging porch steps to her front door, frowning at the deep claw marks and peeling paint. The dog beat her there and nearly knocked her down again as he squeezed past, struggling to be first through the opening. He scrabbled across the wood floor, intent on his food bowl at the back of the house.

"*Hardy.* That's so rude," she said, though she knew he'd probably never care about the finer points of canine behavior. One more item for her list of things to do: check into obedience classes. She'd thought she could handle dog ownership, but they both needed some expert help.

She toed off her boots and left them in the middle of the cluttered front room and then shuffled through the long, narrow dining room and kitchen to the mudroom doorway. "Want your dinner? Do you?"

The dog danced around her, drooling on the chipped linoleum. Dumb question. Obvious answer. At least this part of their relationship was consistent.

"Me, too, Hardy." She sucked in a deep breath and let out a huge sigh. "Wish I had someone to fix it for me." She dumped a scoop of kibble in his bowl and set it outside on the cramped concrete landing above her cracked, uneven patio.

Another project: replacing those ugly concrete squares. A piece of cake for a woman who owned a concrete delivery company. All she needed was a jackhammer to break out the old slab and some help with slapping the forms in place.

And then she should landscape the space beyond with something more imaginative than grass and evergreen shrubs. And plant a tree or two for some contrast against the thick, dark redwood grove beyond her fence—although what kind of landscaping and trees, she had no idea.

Tess would know what would look right. And Addie could help choose the paint for the front door. Thank goodness she had highly trained females for friends.

Hardy shoved his head into his bucket and lapped up his after-dinner drink before dashing back inside, dripping water from his jowls and splashing more against her pants as he passed. She heard a crash in the front room—probably his tail swiping the television remote and her empty soda can to the floor—and then the phone.

She decided to let the answering machine pick up and headed toward her bedroom on the opposite side of the house, tugging her sweatshirt over her head. As she passed through the front room, Jack Maguire's drawl moseyed into the space, and she stopped with her head buried inside the cement-coated fabric as that syrupy voice poured over her, turning her stomach into one big knot. Again.

"Hey there, Charlie. I swung by your plant, and the gate was locked, so I figured you might be home by now."

She pulled off the shirt and dropped it on her over-stuffed chair. "Spying on me, Maguire?"

"Agatha doesn't want this mess of fish I caught filling up her refrigerator, and I can't blame her."

"Bragger," she murmured as she unzipped her jeans.

"I snagged the prettiest little rock cod that reminded me of you—except for the scaly skin and bugged-out eyes. I thought I'd drop it by so you can fry it up for your breakfast tomorrow. It's not catfish, but it'll do. There's nothing like some fresh fish and potatoes cooked with a dash of salt and pepper and a generous slice of butter to start the day off right."

"Ugh." She grimaced as she worked her pants over her hips. "Not a chance."

"But maybe it's just as well you're not home right now. I'll ask Agatha to hold this till later. Then I'll only have to make one trip out to your neck of the woods tonight."

Charlie froze with her jeans around her ankles.

"I'll be there about, oh, say, seven o'clock. We can have ourselves a cozy cocktail party before dinner. Wear something nice, 'cause—"

She kicked her way out of her pants and picked up the phone. "What in the hell are you talking about?"

"Afternoon, Charlie." She could practically hear the smug, satisfied grin in his voice. "Y'see? I thought you'd be home by now, and so you are."

"What do you want, Maguire?"

"I've got a gift for you. A small token of my esteem and appreciation."

"Yeah. I heard. A scaly, bug-eyed fish."

"Wait'll you see her. She's a beauty," he said. "And I'm glad you were listening in—that'll save me time. I'm always in favor of saving time. I like to save it up in great big batches and—"

"Let me save you some right now, Maguire." He'd already wasted too much of hers with that slowpoke meandering around the point. "I'm not having dinner with you."

She'd been prepared to stall things over a casual drink in a public spot. To slow his progress with another dance, if he insisted—although she'd prefer to keep the physical contact to a minimum. But a weekend dinner meant an intense dose of one-on-one time. A long, uninterrupted stretch of tricky conversation with a man who made her blood heat and her mouth go dry every time he flashed those dimples in her direction. She was starting to have second thoughts about these particular business complications.

"Well now, that's a shame," he said. "'Cause I made us a reservation at the finest place in town."

She snorted. "I don't think I trust the judgment of a man who suggests fried fish for breakfast."

"Don't knock it till you've tried it."

"I'm not having dinner with you." She ran a hand through her hair and grimaced at the grime sticking to her fingers. "I've got other plans." Starting with a shower.

"I'm sure you do. A pretty lady like you would have all sorts of plans for a Saturday night."

Obviously his research hadn't been all that thorough. "That's right. And I'd better get started on them. So if you'll excuse me—"

"Of course. Go right ahead, and pardon me for interrupting. There'll be plenty of time later to fill you in on what Sawyer and I discussed today." He paused. "About the future of BayRock, among other things."

Charlie narrowed her eyes.

"Maybe I'll catch up with you sometime next week," he continued. "Thursday or Friday might be good."

"Or you could fill me in right now."

"Sorry, can't do that. I promised Agatha I'd run an errand for her. She'd do it herself, but she's waiting to check in another guest. Besides," he added, "I wouldn't want to keep you from all those plans of yours. Guess I'd better say goodbye and—"

"Wait." Charlie sank into the chair. She knew she was being manipulated, but maybe she could turn the tables on him. *Stalling,* she reminded herself. *Research.* The fact that she wanted to see him again, to have a legitimate excuse to stare at that handsome face and enjoy that tiny buzz when his gaze glided over her had nothing to do with her decision.

Time to deal with things in a calm, rational manner. She took a deep breath and blew out a silent sigh. "I'll cancel my plans and meet you at the restaurant."

"Well now, that's mighty generous of you, Charlie. I want you to know just how much I appreciate your sacrificing some of your personal time to discuss business with me. But you're forgetting one thing."

"What's that?"

"Your fish."

"Right," she said as she rubbed her forehead. "My bug-eyed breakfast."

"I wouldn't want to trouble Agatha for a special container and enough ice to keep my gift fresh in the car while we're enjoying our meal. I'd best drop it off at your place. And while I'm there, you might as well hop in my car for the trip to the restaurant."

"Then you'll have to drive me back."

"It's a company rental, and this is a business meeting."

She recognized that oh-so-reasonable tone, the one that meant he wasn't going to accept *no* for an answer. She'd heard it last night on The Shantyman's dance floor.

This time her sigh was long and loud. "What time will you be here?"

"Seven o'clock. That'll give us time to relax over a cocktail or two. Get the business part of the evening out of the way."

She refrained from pointing out that there'd be no reason

then to continue with dinner after the drinks. Instead, she gave him directions to her house and hung up.

Muttering a string of curses, she collected her discarded clothes, let Hardy into the house to perform shower guard duty and studied the meager supply of nice clothes in her closet. There was only one choice for an evening like this: the basic black dress Tess had shoved at her months ago during a weekend shopping trip to the Bay Area.

She tugged the dress from its hanger, laid it on her bed and headed toward the bathroom to begin preparing for Jack's arrival. Being part owner of a ready-mix business meant brutal hours, big worries, exhausting schedules and messy repairs. But the evening stretching ahead was beginning to rank among the worst tortures she'd faced on the job. Not only would she be forced to navigate the undercurrents of social conversation with a Southern shark while wearing a dress—she'd have to shave her legs.

JACK RESTED HIS PALM AGAINST the back of Charlie's narrow waist as they followed the hostess to one of the linen-covered tables in Avalon's dining room. Her muscles tensed beneath his fingers, and she picked up her pace to step out of reach. He grinned at the predictability of her reaction to his touch. Those flinches and blushes and nasty glances of hers somehow made the occasional social contact much more fun than it already was.

More fun that it should be. His grin dimmed as he reminded himself why he was here. He'd planned to keep her distracted and off balance—and things wouldn't be quite so much fun if his plan turned around and bit him in the butt while he had his eye on hers.

Which was precisely where his gaze happened to be fixed at the moment. Not a bad view at all, now that it was spruced up in a short black dress that highlighted the form and clung to the curves.

The hostess waited patiently while Jack annoyed Charlie by fussing with her chair, and then she handed them their menus and assured them their server would appear shortly. Charlie snapped her napkin into her lap and shot a menacing glance at Jack over the table's candle flickering in its cut-glass bowl. She had such a pretty glare, with flecks of gold in her big gray eyes that coordinated with the glints of copper in her wildly wavy hair.

"I had no idea you were bringing me here," she said with something close to a snarl.

"I told you I was going to treat you to dinner at the nicest place in town."

A pretty blond server approached their table and introduced herself as April. She agreed with him that this was, indeed, the nicest place in town as she filled their water glasses.

"I didn't think you meant *here*," Charlie continued when April had left.

"What's wrong with this place?" Jack made a show of studying their surroundings—one of the parlors in a shipping merchant's mansion which had been cleverly refurbished as an intimate dining area. The high ceiling was frosted with plasterwork and bathed in the mellow light of antique chandeliers, the walls and antiques draped and padded with sumptuous damasks and lavish velvets. A cozy fire glowed in an ornate marble fireplace, and fresh flowers scented the air with a spicy perfume. "Looks nice enough to me."

"This is a private club."

"So I was told when I called for the reservation."

"You couldn't possibly be a member."

"True enough," said Jack with a shrug. "But my employer knows someone who is." He lifted his water glass and sipped. "I hear there's a ballroom upstairs. Maybe you can give me a tour after our meal."

"I've never been in here before."

And wasn't that a shame, he thought as April returned to take his wine order. He'd figured someone with Charlie's connections would have been invited to Avalon for a social occasion or special event, even if she couldn't afford a membership of her own.

"Jack." Mike Drummond, city councilman and owner of the largest construction firm in the county—and one of Keene Concrete's most loyal customers, according to Jack's sources—stopped at the table and gave Jack a friendly slap on the shoulder. "Nice to see you again."

"Evenin', Mike." Jack rose from his seat and shook the hand the contractor offered. "You know my date, don't you?"

Charlie's eyes widened with something akin to panic. "I'm not his date. I'm… He's…"

"Good to see you, Charlie," Mike said, bailing her out. "You're looking—" The contractor broke off as he gave her a second, closer look. He seemed confused by what he saw. "Well."

She blushed beneath her freckles and lowered her lashes at the uncertain compliment.

Folks around here probably didn't quite know what to make of Charlie when she was polished up and wearing clothes that made her look downright womanly. And it was obvious from the tiny tug she gave the dress's swooping neckline that she didn't quite know what to make of herself, either.

And wasn't that another shame, since she was easily the most attractive female in the building. Jack's fingers curled into fists at his sides. What was wrong with the men in this town, anyway? A woman like Charlie shouldn't have been available for a last-minute date on a Saturday night.

"Lovely," said Jack.

Charlie's lashes flickered, and then her gaze lifted to meet his.

"She looks *lovely,*" he repeated.

Mike cleared his throat in the awkward silence that followed Jack's declaration. "Say, Jack, you free for some golf tomorrow?"

With an effort, Jack dragged his gaze from Charlie's blushing face. "Tomorrow?"

Mike nodded. "Ten o'clock tee time? I'm working up a foursome."

"Sounds good." Jack paused, waiting to hear whether Mike would extend a similar invitation to his dinner guest. But it seemed David was the only member of the Keene family who spent any time on the links—or at least the only one who merited an invitation to join an impromptu golf group. "I'll need to borrow some clubs," he added.

"No problem. The pro's got a set stashed away that'll suit you just fine." Mike aimed a finger at him as he walked away. "See you then."

"Right. Thanks, Mike."

Jack smoothed his tie as he sank back into his seat, and then he took a moment to carefully rearrange his napkin and his thoughts. When he was feeling steady again, he glanced up to see that Charlie's familiar glare was already back in place.

"Now what?" he asked.

"Nice to see you again? Free for some golf?"

He shrugged. "I met Mike at a job site yesterday."

"And now you're old friends."

"I'm a friendly guy."

"Yeah. Right. I've noticed."

"Better get used to it, Charlie," said Jack, grinning as he reached for his water glass. "I'm going to be around for a while."

"You're not going to be around long enough for me to change my habits, Maguire."

"You keep reminding me I'm leaving." He leaned forward and lowered his voice to a stage whisper. "Makes me want to say something along the lines of 'Kiss me goodbye, Scarlett, and make it good, 'cause we're about to say farewell forever.'"

That shut her up nice and tight, like a bad-tempered clam. For the moment, at least. She snatched up her menu and scowled at her choices.

Most of which involved seafood, Jack noted when he scanned his own calligraphed card. Fresh, too, he assumed—and from the looks of it, expertly prepared. He could get used to eating like this.

He could get used to friendly backslaps in public places and impromptu invitations to golf games, too. Life in the big city offered more choices for an evening's company or a Sunday morning's entertainment, but all those hundreds of thousands of people could sometimes separate a fellow from the folks he cared for most.

He doubted that happened very often in Carnelian Cove.

Charlie studied him over the edge of her menu with a suspicious frown. "What are you thinking?"

"How pleasant it is around here. How pleasant it must be to live here." Jack leaned back in his seat as their server returned with the wine and began the bottle-opening ritual. "Don't you think this is a pleasant place to live, April?"

"I guess so." She smiled shyly as she twisted the screw into the cork. "Sure."

"That's one vote. What about you, Charlie?"

"Are you taking a poll?"

"Yep," he said, because it was so much fun to tease her. So much easier to keep knocking her off balance than to struggle with finding his own. "Starting tonight."

"Yeah, I think so, too. But not everyone agrees with me," she muttered as she lowered her gaze to her menu.

"David, for instance."

She dismissed her brother with a shrug. "He'll figure things out and settle down soon enough."

"Might help to see some alternatives first." Jack tasted the wine and nodded his approval.

One of Charlie's glossy red curls slipped forward over

her narrow shoulder to brush her collarbone. Jack's lungs seemed to constrict, and he slowly drew his next breath through the pressure building in his chest.

"Helps a man figure out what he's settling for," he said.

Whatever the hell that might be.

CHAPTER EIGHT

LOVELY. SHE LOOKS LOVELY.

Charlie tucked Jack's unexpected words into a mental back pocket and tried to stay focused on their conversation. It was difficult, because she was feeling nearly as beautiful as he'd said she looked. And she simply wasn't equipped to deal with that sensation, to act normally and to say things that made sense when this strange, new Charlie was blooming and buzzing inside her.

She wanted to pull his words back out and linger over their echo. She wanted to take the time to relive and savor those amazing moments, now, before they faded from memory. Her father was the only man who'd ever said such a thing to her, and she'd assumed she'd never hear that compliment from a man again. But she had a difficult evening to get through—a job to do.

Research. She sat very still, waiting, concentrating on Jack's message—something about settling for the inevitable—until her glass was filled and the server had disappeared.

"Have you figured it out?" she asked.

"I'm leaning toward the halibut," said Jack. "I have to admit I'm curious about whether a humble fish fillet gets to putting on airs when it's 'enrobed in a béchamel sauce.'"

"I wasn't talking about dinner." She lifted her glass and tasted the wine—a delicious, velvety Merlot. Everything around her suddenly seemed more vivid. Disconcerting. Interfering with business. "I meant what it is you're settling for."

Jack gave her a strangely intense look—a disconcerting look—and then shook his head. "I don't know if that particular phrase applies in my case," he said. "I don't think I'm settling for anything."

"That's right. You're one of those men who's always making a move."

Making a move.

One of his deeply dimpled smiles began its slow trek across his features, and she silently cursed the warmth washing her cheeks. She hadn't meant to give him an opening to make a move on her. She scowled at him over her glass while she searched for a safer research topic. "All your travel must make it hard to have much of a home."

"That's why I chose a condo in a building with plenty of stay-at-home neighbors who keep an eye on things. Makes it easy to come and go."

"And then there's your accent," she continued after another sip of wine. "You didn't start out from anywhere near here."

"No, ma'am."

"So you've come a long way from where you started," she said, "you're still on the road a lot of the time, and the only permanent home you've got is a piece of someone else's building. And you spend your days snooping around, looking for ways to buy pieces of other people's companies to hand over to someone else."

"Now that's a mighty interesting summary of my life so far." Jack refilled her glass. "And I'd hate to mess with that particular version by pointing out that it's a mite distorted here and there, due to the absence of a few minor but important details. Mostly because I'm curious about the point you're trying to make with that summary in the first place."

"My point is," said Charlie, "that you're in no position to offer someone like David advice on the benefits of seeing the world before he decides what to do with his inheritance. And you have no idea what life in a place like Carnelian Cove is like."

"Now that's one of those important details that pokes some pretty big holes in your summary. And your point, for that matter."

Their server returned, and Jack greeted her as if she were an old family friend. By the time he'd ordered their dinners, he'd discovered April was a part-time college student from Salinas who was living with her boyfriend and studying marine biology.

"Why do you do that?" asked Charlie.

"Ask about the dessert specials before I decide on my dinner?"

"Talk to people the way you do. Anyone. Everyone."

"I told you," he said as he picked up his glass, "I'm a friendly guy."

And so he was, she realized. One of the most sincerely friendly people she'd ever met.

A great guy to have a drink with. Someone who had some interesting stories to tell. Someone to try to understand better so she could figure out how to lessen the damage he was sure to cause.

"Tell me about yourself, Jack," she said. "Tell me why you're such a friendly guy."

"I think I could make a start on that and provide you with one of those important little details you're missing all at once." He folded back the cover on the basket of bread and passed it to her. "It so happens I grew up in a town a whole lot smaller than this one."

"In the south?"

"That's right. I'm the only son of a small-time mechanic working in a small-time shop. My daddy taught me everything I know about using a tool, and my mama taught me how to find my way around a kitchen and sew a button on my shirt. And when I graduated from school, I kissed them both goodbye and headed out to make my fortune in the world."

It sounded as though he'd recited his touching speech before. Several times. She could nearly hear the twang of a fiddle accompanying that drawl. But she thought she'd detected a hint of regret beneath the practiced words, something shadowy behind his carefully shuttered expression. "Are they still there? Your parents?"

He hesitated for several long moments, and then he shook his head. "My mother died of cancer the year after I left, and my father took to drinking. One of the neighbors found him in a field, pinned under his tractor. The coroner told me he didn't suffer long."

"I'm sorry."

"I appreciate the sympathy." He stared into his glass as he twisted the stem. "Family ties can be either a blessing or a curse, I s'pose."

"I suppose I should be grateful for mine."

He raised his glass with a grin. "To family ties, and all the s'posin' that comes along with them."

She managed a tentative smile as she tipped her glass against his. His candor made him seem less formidable, somehow. Slightly sympathetic, perhaps.

And much more attractive, damn it.

Charlie sipped her wine and set her glass aside as April arrived with the first course and a wide smile for her favorite customer. He was still dangerous, and as slippery as a catfish in a bucket of oil, but Jack Maguire was indeed a friendly guy—and an interesting person to have a drink with.

Two hours later, after a second bottle of wine and a meandering tour of Avalon's sumptuous rooms, Charlie was feeling precariously agreeable—though her wobbly high heels may have had something to do with the precarious part. Odd how her balance had deteriorated along with her objections to Jack's presence in her life, she thought as she stumbled over a dip in the pavement on the walk to his car.

He grabbed her by the arm, and she tried to shrug him off, but he gave her that raised-eyebrow look of his and tightened his grip. She'd only known him a couple of days, but it was obvious Jack didn't have a lot of experience with taking no for an answer. Not the kind of fact she'd intended her research to reveal, perhaps, but handy to know.

A gust of wind from the north swept her hair from her face, and she breathed in the sharp wintry air as if it were a tonic, hoping to to clear her mind and her senses. She tugged her lightweight woolen wrap more tightly about her shoulders.

"Thanks for dinner," she said as he pulled his keys from his pocket. "It was…nice."

"Nice?" He shifted toward her, and the grooves bracketing his mouth deepened with amusement.

"Yes." She rearranged the folds of her wrap around her shoulders, searching for something else to say. It was difficult to continue the small talk with his eyes so intent on hers. "The food was very good."

"Good?"

He tipped forward another inch, and she drew back, wincing when the handle of his car door poked against her hip. "Yes," she said. "Very."

"Very?"

He lifted a hand toward her face, and she froze, her pulse hammering and her breath catching. *Lovely. She looks lovely.*

He paused, and his eyebrows dipped in the hint of a frown, and then he skimmed a finger down her cheek and along her jaw—a slow tease of a touch—and tipped up her chin. She wanted to turn her head and duck out of range, but her intentions short-circuited in a warm flood of shimmery sensations.

"Yes. Very," she said. The words came out in a tiny croak, and she swallowed. "Wh-what are you doing?"

"Getting ready to kiss you."

Yes. Oh, yes. "Why?"

He edged toward her again, and one of his legs brushed against one of hers. "Why not?"

She knew she should raise her hand between them and push him away, but her arm seemed as shaky and tingly and weak as the rest of her body. "You're not thinking you can seduce me out of the deal, are you?"

"Hmm." His gaze swept over her features. "I'll admit I may have considered the possibility of seducing you just for the fun of it. But if I can cut you out of the deal by taking you to bed…"

He'd thought about seducing her? This gorgeous man had actually had those kinds of thoughts—about her?

Lovely…lovely…

"You wouldn't dare," she said.

"Take you to bed?"

"Try to cut me out of the deal that way."

He smiled and stroked his thumb across her chin, and she stifled a gasp. "Are you daring me to do it?" he asked.

"Would you try it if I did?"

"I don't take dares, as a rule. Too risky." He shifted closer. "But we could agree to give it a try and see what happens."

"Figures a tactic like that might appeal to a man like you."

His chuckle was warm and low and seemed to rumble right through her. "You have a very low opinion of me, don't you?"

"It balances out the one you've got on the other end of the scale."

His gaze dropped to her mouth as he traced her lower lip with his thumb. She imagined his mouth replacing his fingertip, his tongue skimming along that same line, and she nearly melted at his feet in a puddle of lust. It had been far too long since a man had paid her this kind of attention—and none of the men in her past had had quite this syrupy, sensual way about them.

"You can't sucker me on this deal, Maguire," she said. Could he feel her trembling?

"Probably not," he said. "I've never considered doing business in this particular manner before." He edged still closer. "I think I might like it."

"You can't, you know."

"Seduce you?" He slid his arm around her waist, beneath the soft wool draped over her back. "Or cut you out of the deal?"

"Either," she said, her voice faint. "Both."

"Make up your mind, Charlie." He pulled her against him. "I'm getting some mixed signals here."

"That's your problem."

"Mmm." His long, lean fingers fanned across her back. "I like having a problem I can deal with."

He pressed his lips to the side of her neck. Warm, moist silk edged with stubble. She shivered again at the feel of his mouth on her skin and prayed her trembling body wouldn't shatter into a million pieces and swirl away on the next puff of icy air.

"Can you?" he asked.

"Can I what?" Her eyes drifted closed.

"Deal with it."

She tilted her head to the side to give him more room and encouragement to keep doing whatever fabulous thing he was doing to her earlobe. "I can deal with anything you can, Maguire."

He lifted his head and waited for her to meet his gaze. "This ought to be interesting, then."

There, in his eyes, was desire. *For her*. She was sure of it. A heady, delicious, feminine thrill coiled through her, and she wrapped her fingers around his lapels. She shouldn't be doing this—it wasn't smart, and it wasn't safe. He was only toying with her, testing her, pushing her buttons—but he still wanted to kiss her. *Her*. And she wanted to kiss him right back, so much she was willing to ignore all the warnings buzzing in her head and let him get away with it, just this once.

She closed her eyes to blot out the image of the man who made her heart race with a combination of attraction and terror. And then she waited, trembling, for that first contact of mouth to mouth, breath to breath. There had been so few first kisses in her life, and she'd savored the anticipation of each and every one—the tingling excitement, the unnerving intimacy, the dizzying hope.

He didn't disappoint her.

CHAPTER NINE

CHARLIE SIMPLY SURRENDERED to the miracle of Jack's kiss. The night breeze eddied around her ankles, and the scents of cologne and wood smoke mingled in the clinging mist, and the shadows beyond the parking lot security light seemed to swallow the *whoosh* of a passing car. She knew where she was and what she was doing; she knew she should end it, and soon, but she was quickly forgetting why.

This wasn't the kiss of a man who was taking her measure in some sort of cat-and-mouse business move. His hand stroked up her spine, and his fingers slid into her hair to fist at her nape, and his breath caught and quickened, and she tasted his surprise and delight, and she knew he was no longer toying and testing, that he was lost with her in the pleasure of the moment.

And in the next moment, something snapped and flared between them, something dark and exciting, and he was no longer the laid-back charmer who'd cheerfully admitted his ulterior motives. He tightened his grip and crushed her against him, and his tongue swept into her mouth, and a deep groan rumbled from his chest and seemed to vibrate through her.

Lovely, lovely.

She matched his urgency with her own, nipping at his lip and shoving her hands beneath his jacket to spread her fingers over the heated fabric of his thin dress shirt, clawing at his back, daring him to take her higher. His mouth scraped over hers in a demanding caress, and she strained against him, reckless with the realization that this man—this attractive, intelligent, aggravating man—was as aroused as she was.

His hands streaked over her as he bore down, pressing her against the car, fastening his mouth on her neck, grinding his hips against hers, and she shuddered and grasped his hair and dragged him back, back for another greedy kiss while she tried to blot out the realization that she was practically devouring the man who made her temper spike with his relentless pursuit of his goals and his single-minded determination to have his way and—

And his threat to her family and her livelihood.

SOMEWHERE ALONG THE RAGGED edges of Jack's awareness, he felt a tremor pass through Charlie, and he cursed the cold and his selfishness. Her bare legs were exposed to the evening breeze, and her thin, sleeveless dress provided scant insulation beneath her light wrap. He lowered his hands to her waist and edged back, but the look in her eyes made him sorry he'd decided to be so chivalrous.

"I want you," he said.

She stilled—a tiny, telling pause—and then she trailed her fingers down his spine. "Well, you can't have me."

"You want me, too." He rubbed his hands up her arms. "Don't try to deny it."

"Why would I?" Her gaze was steady on his. The uncertainty that had beguiled him had been transformed into a wariness that challenged him.

He lifted a hand and combed his fingers through her hair. Wild, silky waves and curls of lush, beautiful red. "Because you like arguing with me."

"No, I don't."

He smiled and lowered his forehead to hers. God, she smelled wonderful. "You just proved my point."

"You make it hard to carry on a conversation when you turn everything into some kind of competition."

"Then shut up and stick your tongue down my throat again."

"I did not. I—"

He silenced her with another deep, drugging kiss, spinning it out, leaving them both breathless. "There you go again," he murmured. "Arguing."

She tortured him by tickling her fingertips along his jaw and down his neck. "Maybe this is a good place to stop and say good night," she said.

He captured her fingers and gave them a gentle squeeze. "You can't quit now."

"Watch me," she said as she pulled her hand from his.

He inhaled deeply and backed away—away from the insanity of the past several minutes. "All right, then. I'll drive you home and see you to your door."

"No point in arguing, I suppose." She stepped aside and he opened her door for her.

"Go ahead," he said as she slid into the car. "Argue all you want."

But she didn't argue. She sat, silent and brooding, clutching her bag in her lap and staring out the passenger window at the amber porch lights and quaint silhouettes of Carnelian Cove neighborhoods they passed.

Jack had been blessed with a nimble mind and a clever tongue, tools he counted on to wiggle out of sticky situations. So the fact that he found himself struggling for a conversation starter was both a damn uncomfortable sensation and a blow to his pride.

He considered turning on some music to cut through the awkward silence in the car, and then he cursed his hesitation over the selection. Mozart or Motown—anything would be better than listening to the whispers of his guilty conscience.

He shifted in his seat, uncomfortable with the way he'd anticipated Charlie's reactions better than he'd estimated his own. It had been obvious, since that first moment they'd met in her office, that she was one part attracted and two parts curious. He'd figured that curiosity of hers would be enough to tip her into trouble, and that he'd be able to figure out some way to knock her completely off balance and into his arms.

What he hadn't figured on was the way she'd feel in his arms once she'd landed there. He hadn't given any thought to the possible effects of that firecracker sizzle of hers or the amazing way it all kind of smoothed out in a deliciously distilled punch when she melted against him, all subtle curves and soft flesh. He hadn't planned on enjoying kissing her as much as he had—and he didn't like surprises, especially when they were surprises about himself.

He'd suspected Charlie was uncertain of her allure and inexperienced with the opposite sex; he'd seen the evidence in every flinch and shrug. Her intriguing combination of toughness and vulnerability, her stubborn strength encased in that soft body, the shock that flickered in her eyes as he'd lowered his face toward hers had warned him off and drawn him in at the same time. If he wasn't careful, she'd ending up seducing him while he was trying to seduce her.

Is that what he'd been doing—trying to seduce her? It would be a risky move, even for a man who thrived on the edgy jolt of a good gamble. He had too much to lose—his secure footing in a slippery corporate world, the chance for a promotion, the sweet satisfaction of snatching another victory away from Noah, his current rival at Continental. And he'd told this woman more about himself than he'd intended, blurting out the story of his parents' deaths. Had he ever shared that so easily with a relative stranger? He felt raw and exposed, as if she'd peeled away a thin layer of his skin.

He stole a glance in her direction. He wondered if she was having the same kinds of arguments with herself that he was having, and then he wondered if they'd have more fun arguing over the matter together. Probably. He liked arguing with her almost as much as he liked kissing her.

He simply liked Charlie, whether he was arguing with her or kissing her or not. But did he like her well enough to further complicate a tricky deal? He doubted he'd have the time to find out, and he wouldn't hurt her by rushing into something that neither of them could finish.

With a heavy dose of regret and an odd sense of loss, he turned into her drive and pulled the key from the ignition. She unbuckled her seat belt, and he reached for her hand and curled his fingers over hers. "I'll see you to your door, like I promised."

"Of course." She freed her hand and brushed the strap aside with a frown. "I'm sure that's how you end all your business dinners."

He followed her along the narrow walkway to her front porch, through the unworldly shadows of the tall trees rimming her yard. Above them, a few ice-chip stars winked through ribbony clouds moving across the full moon. He stepped to the porch's edge and waited behind her, near the railing, while she fumbled through her handbag, digging for her key. He stared at the abstract remains of a spider's web outlined in the amber glow of the porch light, trying to ignore the scent of her shampoo and the fact that her wrap had slipped to one side, exposing her pale, smooth skin.

When he heard her mutter a curse, he considered snatching the purse from her and finding that damn key himself. Instead, he grabbed a fold of her wrap and tugged it over her bare shoulder. His knuckles brushed her cool skin, and his fingers fisted in the soft fabric. And with a silent curse of his own he lost his slim grip on his self-control and leaned in to nuzzle the sweet, tempting spot beneath her earlobe. "I like your house," he whispered. *I like you. So very much.*

She froze with the key in her hand. "It needs a lot of work."

"Just think of all the possibilities." He slid his hands

around her waist and pulled that curvy, compact butt of hers against his hips.

"It's full of junk," she said in a breathy voice.

"One man's junk is another man's treasure." He leaned in close and gently pried the key from her fingers, taking the opportunity to press his lips to the tender slope of her neck before sliding the key into the slot.

She closed her hand over his, twisted the knob and pushed the door open. "It's got a—"

A streak of black shot past her and hit him a few vulnerable inches below the belt. *Hard.*

He clutched at the front of his pants and doubled over, staggered back and flipped over the low porch railing, landing on his back in the middle of her cold, damp patch of weeds. The impact knocked the wind out of him, the shocking pain nearly distracting him from his throbbing crotch. Something heavy and furry attacked his face with a slithery, slimy tongue.

Her dog. The seventy-pound terror that had pounced and shoved him against the wall when he'd arrived to escort her to dinner. The slobbering hoodlum that had left a dark smudge on his dress pants, knocked over a lamp and scattered a stack of magazines in his welcoming rampage.

Jack struggled to suck in some air so he could curl up and die in the fetal position.

"*Hardy.* Down. *Down.*" Charlie scrambled down the steps. "Get down."

"He is *down,*" said Jack with a grunt as he shoved at the canine mugger. "If he got any lower, he'd be under the ground."

"Sorry about this." She tried to get a grip on the dog, but he whirled out of reach and landed on Jack again, getting in another couple of sloppy licks. "He hasn't learned how to greet strangers yet."

"This is a mighty effective approach." Jack rolled away from the dog, which quickly came at his face from a different angle. "Makes an immediate impression."

"Hardy." She managed to grab his collar and dragged him away. "Okay, I've got him."

"Thank God." Jack shut his eyes and collapsed back on the crumpled weeds, rubbing his sleeve across his face while she asked her poor widdle boy whether mean ol' Jack had hurt the doggie's feelings. Obviously there was one man in Charlie's life who enjoyed the privilege of seeing her softer side.

He staggered to his feet, breathing heavily, and hunched over to rest his hands on his knees.

"Are you all right?" asked Charlie.

"Fine. Just fine."

"Would you like to come in for some coffee or something?"

"Or something?" He straightened gingerly, keeping a close watch on the dog whining at her side. Shame about his manners—he sure was a good-looking animal.

"Tea?" she asked.

He gazed at her, at the big round eyes so dark against her moonlit face, at her anxious expression and her small, slender form and the pretty wrap dragging on the damp ground. He was staring again, and he didn't care.

"Water?" she asked.

"Water?"

"You know—water." She ran a hand through her hair in a nervous gesture. "It comes out of the tap."

He shook his head. "I'm going to leave now—"

"I'm sorry about Hardy, I—"

"—because I want to stay. Entirely too much."

"Oh," she said uncertainly. "Okay, then."

"No." He shook his head again. "It's not okay, Charlie."

He chanced a step closer to her and hesitated when Hardy strained against his collar. "I want you," he told her. "More than ever."

Her shoulders lifted and fell on a long, loud sigh. "You're right. It's not okay."

"And you want me."

"I…" She paused for a long moment and then pressed her lips together in a tight frown. "This isn't a good idea."

"You're probably right. But I want to be sure." He released the breath he hadn't realized he'd been holding, waiting for her answer. "What's wrong?" He edged closer, wanting to see what was in her eyes. "No argument this time?"

"I don't know what to do about…" She waved a hand in a vague circle. "About this."

"Neither do I. But I know what to do about it tonight."

He slowly closed the gap between them and let Hardy have a quick, moist sniff at his fingers before he settled a hand on the dog's head. "I'm going to kiss your mistress good-night now, Hardy," he said as he rubbed behind the dog's ear. "A short, sweet good-night kiss. The kind of kiss that avoids any complications that may be waiting down the road."

He leaned in, slowly, and paused, waiting through several moments of chest-squeezing suspense and heady anticipation, until she lifted her face to his, and then he gently pressed his lips to hers. The dog whined and shifted on his haunches, but he stayed in place.

"You see?" Jack whispered against her lips. "Progress."

"If you say so," she muttered.

He laughed as he turned and walked to his car. He'd let her have the last word tonight. He could afford to be generous. He felt so light he was sure he could fly to the tops of those tall, tall trees and keep on going until he zipped right past that fat, white moon.

Besides, he planned on having the last word the next time they met.

AGATHA ALLEN'S SUNDAY morning breakfast spread was an impressive sight to behold. Fancy trays displaying fancier pastries, steaming containers stuffed with scrambled eggs, fat sausages and herbed potatoes, plates of sliced melon arranged in clever spirals—and a few fillets of one of the fish he'd given her, lightly dusted with flour and fried a perfect golden brown. But it was the aroma of her fresh coffee that most interested Jack, since this morning he felt the need for some caffeine to help get him through eighteen holes on the golf course.

He heaped his plate with generous portions and took a place at the long table set with lacy linen and bright blue irises fanned out of a crystal vase. The other guests—a retired couple from Idaho and a trio of kayakers heading up the coast to Oregon—chatted about the sites they'd visited before drifting away to prepare for another day of exploration.

Agatha swung through the kitchen door. "More coffee, Jack?"

"Yes, thank you." He held his cup while she poured. "Why don't you sit down and join me for a while?"

She paused to consider her answer, obviously weighing her disapproval of his business against her desire for his continued goodwill toward her own. "All right."

She selected one of the dainty china cups arranged on the buffet and sat across the table. "What's your tee time?"

"Ten." He forked up another bite of fish. "It's going to be a long stretch till lunch."

"Don't worry—Mike won't let you starve." She added a dash of cream to her coffee. "And here I thought you'd piled your plate so high because you like my cooking."

"I do at that." He slathered butter on a raisin-flecked muffin. "I've gotten mighty spoiled during the past couple of days. Particularly by those apple fritters you made on Friday," he hinted.

"Maybe I'll make some again this week. An extra-large batch." She sipped her coffee and stared out the window. "Looks like you'll have a clear day for your round of golf."

"Looks like." He settled back in his chair and stretched his legs beneath the table. He'd miss Agatha and these morning visits, prickly as they were at times. He'd miss the shifting scents of fishing gear and dairy barns, the muffled clangs of the buoys in the harbor and the mournful lowing of the cows in the fields. He could feel the peace of the place seeping into him, slowing his pace.

It was downright unnerving. Enough to make a fellow a mite unhinged, which would serve as a convenient explanation for his crazy behavior the previous evening. Throwing him off his stride, distracting him from his goals. Getting him knocked on his butt—literally.

"How was your dinner at Avalon last night?" asked Agatha. "You got back pretty late."

"Waiting up for me?"

"That's not included in the price of the room," she answered with a bland look. "I happened to be out late myself and noticed your car was gone when I got back."

She lowered her cup to the table and smoothed a wrinkle in the cloth. "So, did you and Charlie have a good time?"

"I can't answer for Charlie, but I enjoyed the evening. Very much."

"She seems a little tough on the outside," said Agatha, "but those of us who know her well know she can be kind-hearted when it matters."

"She appears to be an interesting woman." He dabbed at his mouth with an embroidered napkin as he sought to change the topic. "What do folks around here do on a Sunday morning in February?"

"The usual. Go to church, visit with family. Walk on the beach or sail on the bay if the weather's nice enough, or go for a drive through one of the parks. There are a few shops open along Main Street and not too many tourists clogging them at this time of year. Excuse me," she said as she rose from the table to answer the phone ringing in her kitchen.

He stared out the window and considered poking

through more of those shops near the marina. Or hiking along one of the park trails the bicyclists had mentioned. He was curious what he'd find among the ferns and shadows beneath the redwoods.

"Jack?" Agatha stood in the kitchen doorway, staring at him with a puzzled expression. "There's a phone call for you. It's Geneva Chandler."

He'd heard of Carnelian Cove's leading citizen, of course. Anyone who'd spent any time here would hear her name spoken or note it on a dedication plaque. And anyone who'd done any research on the area would learn about the Chandler clan and its influence on local affairs.

He folded the fussy napkin and set it beside his plate as he stood. "Do you have an extension?"

"You can use the phone in the kitchen." Agatha shifted to the side to let him pass. "I don't mind."

Of course not. She'd be listening to his every word as she did the dishes.

CHAPTER TEN

NORMALLY MAUDIE APPRECIATED Ben's company at her weekly church service. Although she found comfort in her volunteer activities and enjoyed socializing with her friends, she'd dreaded facing those interminable Sunday-morning coffee hours by herself after Mitch had died. Now she once again formed half of a twosome, and the security of Ben's presence compensated for his disinterest in shifting their relationship beyond the sweetly affectionate phase. It was probably for the best. His apathy was a good match for her ambivalence.

She tensed when he moved one of his long, slender hands from the steering wheel of his car and placed it over one of hers.

"What's wrong?" he asked. "You haven't said a word since we left church."

"I've had a lot on my mind lately." Maudie turned her head to stare out the passenger window and focus on the changes spring was bringing to the familiar views of her neighborhood. Spikes of grape hyacinth crowded the planters in Grace Spetzler's yard, and creamy buds were opening on the bare branches of Angela Hawley's spreading magnolia. "Sometimes I like to block it all out and simply enjoy the day."

"I suppose that's a good strategy for a Sunday." Ben gave her hand a reassuring pat and then placed his back on the steering wheel. "Monday will be here soon enough."

Which meant he'd be pressing her tomorrow for a decision about making an offer on BayRock—and its effects on her children and Keene Concrete.

She'd considered those effects, again, after they'd all left her house on Friday night. And then she'd taken her calculator and gone over her figures. Twice. She'd always liked numbers. She liked the way they lined up in neat, logical columns—unlike everything else in her life.

"I don't have to punch a time card," she said.

"That's right." He made a smooth, easy turn into her drive. "But the rest of us do."

She stared at the daffodils springing up in clumps around the base of her naked maple and clasped her hands in her lap. "It sounds like it's more important than ever that I make the right decision. I wouldn't want to make the wrong one and be responsible for putting Mitch's company out of business."

"Mitch isn't around anymore," Ben said quietly, and she shut her eyes against the familiar combination of old grief and fresh guilt. She understood and accepted Ben's annoyance when she mentioned Mitch. But she couldn't help it sometimes. Her thirty-three-year habit was proving a tough one to break.

"Keene Concrete belongs to your children now," Ben continued. "And to you."

"I never wanted it, not like this," she said as she pulled her purse into her lap. "And you know I don't know what to do with the part I've got."

"Then sell it."

Maudie stared at him in surprise and dread as he got out of the car and walked around to open her door. Ben had convinced her to sit tight through David's pressure to sell and Charlie's scheme to expand. Why had he suddenly changed his mind?

Did Jack Maguire's arrival in town signify more of a threat than Charlie realized?

Ben extended his hand to help her out of the car. "May I come in for a few minutes? We need to talk."

Maudie nodded and led the way to the house. Her face heated as he took the key from her and unlocked the front door. Her neighbors probably imagined that she and Ben found some interesting ways to pass their Sunday afternoons alone together. But she wouldn't ask him to leave. She'd rather tolerate the gossip than face the long, empty afternoon without him.

"Would you like some coffee?" she asked as they stepped inside.

"No, thank you." He followed her into the front room. "I drank enough after the service to last me the rest of the day."

He shoved his hands into his pockets and stared out her wide front window. The late-morning sunlight seemed to reach through the glass with the sole purpose of polishing the silver in his hair and highlighting the masculine lines of his profile. She caught her breath, as she so often did, at the sight of his tall, lean frame and craggy features. He'd been a gangly boy with a long, bony face; he'd grown into a handsome man.

She'd always harbored a secret crush on Jimmy Stewart—maybe that was part of Ben's appeal.

"Is there something else you'd like to drink?" she asked. "Some water? Juice?"

"You don't have to play the hostess, Maudie." He turned to face her. "And just this once, I'd like to skip playing the guest."

"All right." She sank into her usual chair, easing against the soft cushions covered with plump chintz roses and trailing ivy. "You said we need to talk."

He cleared his throat. "Charlie called me with some interesting information yesterday afternoon. I spent the rest of the day making a few calls of my own, checking out Continental."

Her daughter had called Ben instead of her. Charlie had chosen to discuss business with her mother's financial adviser instead of with her mother. Maudie's own daughter didn't have enough trust, enough belief in her—didn't know her well enough, or care enough—to try to talk things through before turning to someone outside the family.

And why would Charlie consider turning to her mother first, for anything? Mitch had always been there, at the center of things, running the show, providing all the answers. And now that he was gone…there was Ben.

It hurt—oh, how it hurt to think her daughter thought so little of her and what she had to offer. And yet what had she offered these past couple of years but a shallow imitation of Mitch: a weak placeholder at the family's center, a silent buffer between a battling brother and sister. How had she let things reach this point?

"Has something changed?" she asked Ben.

"There's a rumor of a buyout."

"BayRock?"

"Continental." He jiggled the change in his pocket and began to pace. "There's an offer on the table. Geneva's sources in the Bay Area confirmed it."

"Someone is buying Continental? Then why is Jack Maguire here?" Maudie shook her head in confusion. Ever since that man arrived in town, everything had changed. Charlie had grown more tense, more distant. David had holed up in his ramshackle studio—he hadn't even bothered to return her last phone call. And Ben…something seemed different there, too.

She glanced up to see him studying her intently. "Why would Jack Maguire be looking into buying a company when his own is up for sale?" she asked.

"Business has to proceed as usual in a case like this."

"Seems like it would just make things more difficult," she said with another shake of her head. "Continental might be right in the middle of a deal up here. Wouldn't that make an awful mess for the company that buys it? And if the deal fell through, that might mess things up in the Cove, too. It doesn't seem right. Or fair."

"It's business," said Ben with a faint smile.

"I don't much care for business. Not that aspect of it, anyway."

"I know." Ben's smile widened. "You've made that abundantly clear for the past several months."

"Well, I don't," she said, wincing at the petulant tone of her voice. "That's why I don't want any part of it."

"Then sell it."

"Keene Concrete? To Continental?"

"If Maguire offers."

She suddenly grew very, very cold. "Would he?"

"It's a possibility. If I were Maguire, I wouldn't make an offer for BayRock without first seeing what the Keenes might accept. And I'm sure he's one step ahead of us. He's a sharp businessman. A businessman working for a large, successful company."

Maudie raised one eyebrow. "You've met him?"

"No." Ben settled into a chair. "But I've heard of him."

"But what if he does make an offer? You said we might not get much for it."

"Not as much as David's hoping for, anyway. Especially not under the present circumstances."

"Which means none of us would get much." She sighed and rubbed her forehead. "I couldn't do that to Charlie. She just took on that mortgage. And you know what the company means to her."

"Then don't."

Maudie shot a dark look at Ben. "You're no help at all."

"I'm playing a new role today." He folded his hands across his lap. "Today I'm playing your very special friend."

"I don't want your friendship. I want your advice."

"You've had plenty. From me, from Charlie, from David. And from Geneva, I suspect. Now you need to decide what to do with it."

"I'm not sure I have all the facts I need to make a decision yet." Facts that Charlie had chosen to discuss with the man sitting across the room from her. Maudie twisted the rings on her fingers, caught between common sense and wounded pride.

"The Continental rep just might give you a deadline." Ben straightened and leaned toward her. "At the very least, he's going to narrow your options. Might be a good idea to make that decision while you've still got some space to maneuver."

She rubbed again at the spot on her temple where a headache was brewing. "I think I'm going to make some coffee after all."

Ben reached for her arm as she passed. "You can't run from this, Maudie."

"Don't worry." She pulled away and headed for her kitchen, feeling every one of her fifty-one years dragging at her heels. "I'm not going to duck out the back door."

He followed her and paused in the doorway. "Talk to me, Maudie."

"I'm so—" She bit off the *damn* that threatened to leap out and shock them both. "So *tired* of being caught in the middle. All these years, making peace between Mitch and David, between Mitch and Charlie, between Charlie and David. Always smoothing things over. No one ever asked what I wanted. No one ever considered I might have something to contribute. I'm—"

She paused again, mortified by the rush of hot tears that filmed her vision, and sniffed them back. "I'm out of practice. It's been so long since I had to think for myself. To stand up for myself."

Ben stepped into the room and cradled her shoulders in his big hands. "You used to be pretty good at it, too."

"Oh, I was a real hell-raiser in my day." Maudie choked

her way through a bitter laugh. "Got in plenty of trouble for some of the opinions I used to spout at every turn."

"I used to enjoy watching you spout off." He ran his hands down her arms and back to her shoulders again. "You were such a pretty little thing. Noisy and tough, and cute as the dickens."

"Well, I grew up and learned some manners."

"A pity." Ben pulled her into one of his oversize hugs. "I miss that girl sometimes."

"So do I." Maudie closed her eyes and searched for the comfort she usually found in his arms. So different from Mitch's embrace, but so very dear.

"I still see that girl every once in a while," said Ben. "A trace of her, anyway."

Beneath her ear his voice rumbled deep in his chest, a comforting vibration. "You do?"

"Yes." He shifted back and gazed down at her. "I see her every time your daughter gets fired up in the middle of an argument."

Maudie closed her eyes. "I was never that strong."

"You were never that confident. There's a difference. And you've helped build Charlie's confidence every time you've stepped back and let her argue."

He lifted his hands to her face and rubbed his thumbs along her cheeks as if he were brushing aside invisible tears. "You're a good mother, Maudie. That's one of the most important jobs of all, and no businessman, no matter how brilliant he might be, could possibly match it."

"I—" Something was stirring inside her, tucked between the frustration and the panic.

She glanced up at Ben's face, at his searching expression, and she had trouble catching her breath. Suddenly it seemed as if he was standing too close. Why was he standing so close? She shut her eyes again. "Thank you," she managed at last.

"You're welcome."

He moved his lips over hers, as gently and patiently as always. Why did that sweet, affectionate touch irritate her so much today?

She broke away. "I'm sorry, Ben."

He slipped his hands into his pockets. "What are you apologizing for this time?"

"I—" She shook her head. "I guess I'm out of sorts."

"So you said."

"Maybe you'd better leave."

"Is that what you want?" He stepped close again, crowding her. "Do you want me to go? Is that what you want?"

"No." She shoved her hands through her hair, frustrated with him, with the business, with her life in general. It would be so easy to send him away—and he'd go without an argument—but then she'd face another long afternoon with only her miserable self for company. "No, I don't."

"What do you want, Maudie?"

"I want—" She dropped her hands. "I don't know anymore." She turned away and twisted the tap to make coffee that neither of them wanted to drink. She shut off the water and grasped the edge of the sink. "I used to think I wanted everything back the way it was. But it's been too long now, and…I don't. Not anymore."

"I'm glad to hear it."

"Are you?" She spun to face him. "Why? What do you want, Ben? The old Maudie? Is that why you've been hanging around all these months? Waiting to see if she'll make a miraculous appearance?"

"Well, now." He smiled. "Hello, *Maudie*."

Her cheeks heated. "I'm s—"

"Stop." He placed a finger over her lips. "Don't you dare apologize again. I'm tired of your apologies."

"You are?" she whispered behind his hand.

"*Yes*. Yes, I am."

He drew his finger down, slowly, over her mouth, tracing her lower lip. "Ask me again."

Her face was on fire. If she hadn't already finished with the nasty business, she'd have sworn she was having a hot flash. "Ask you what?"

"What it is I want."

Her heart pounded so hard, so fast. "What do you want, Ben?"

"I want to make love to you. Now. This afternoon."

"You do?" She swallowed. "Why?"

"I think we've both been stuck in this loop long enough. Your confusion. My hesitation. Your apologies. My patience." He dropped his finger lower, teasing along the side of her neck, leaving sparks in its wake. "I'm not feeling quite so patient at the moment."

"Mmm." Her eyes drifted closed. She was feeling a little impatient herself.

"Don't you know how much I've been wanting to make love to you all these months?" he asked.

"You have?"

"God, yes." He pulled her close and lowered his mouth to hers again. But this time she could sense the urgency behind the tenderness, the impatient desire simmering beneath the stroke of his fingers over her breast.

"Have you?" he asked.

"Have I been wanting you to hurry up and make your move?"

His chuckle was a warm buzz against her cheek. "Not the exact reply I was hoping for, but it'll do."

She wrapped her arms around his neck and let his caresses carry her away from her worries and her doubts, let his passion help her rediscover the girl who could raise a little hell.

And then she let him take her by the hand and lead her to her room, where the two of them spent the afternoon indulging in more pleasurable activities than the neighbors could possibly imagine.

CHARLIE DUMPED THREE spoonfuls of sugar into her diner coffee Monday morning and silently rehearsed the points she planned to make in this morning's discussion—and the order in which she needed to make them. She pressed a hand to her churning stomach and stared at the view beyond her booth window, battling an attack of insecurity about her ability to manage Keene business. Outside, a fishing boat motored past one of the channel markers, headed for the open ocean.

"Morning, Charlie." Earl slid into the bench seat opposite her.

"Hey there, Earl. Thanks for coming."

She waited while a waitress filled his cup and then nodded toward the boat disappearing into the fog. "How was the fishing trip?"

"Cold." Earl added cream to his coffee. "Next time I'll wait for summer."

"Heard you hooked some big ones."

"Yep." He took a sip and leaned back with a sigh. "Got enough in my freezer to last awhile, that's for sure."

She waited, but he didn't offer more details. Just as well—she didn't want to talk about fishing. "Guess you got along pretty well with that rep from Continental."

"Jack?" Earl opened the menu and studied it. "Well enough."

"He seems like a friendly guy. Considering."

Earl eyed her over the top of the menu. "Considering?"

"Considering what he's up to." She ran a finger along her cup handle. "Feeling us out and all."

"What do you mean, 'us'?"

"He met with David the same day he met with you last week."

"Yeah, he mentioned that." Earl shrugged and dropped the menu back in its slot behind the salt and pepper shakers. "Said it was standard procedure. Checking out the market."

"And playing us off against each other."

Earl picked up his coffee and sipped. "Keene isn't for sale."

"Everything's for sale at the right price. Or under the right circumstances."

He slowly lowered his cup. "Why would Continental

bother to come up with enough money to tempt you to sell out when they can get BayRock for less?"

"Why would they need BayRock if they could get Keene Concrete? You're going to retire soon, anyway."

"Keene isn't for sale," Earl repeated.

"It might be, if Continental's going to be the new competition in town."

She crossed her arms on the table and leaned forward. "I'm not afraid of a little healthy competition. It's good for business, and it's good for Carnelian Cove. It's kept us both on our toes for several years."

"It's kept prices too low." Earl aimed a bony finger at her. "I'd have more in savings to retire on by now."

Their waitress returned, and Charlie asked for her favorite—blueberry pancakes and extra syrup. Earl ordered a Hangtown fry and hash browns.

"Like I said," Charlie continued, "I don't mind some competition. But I don't want to go up against Continental. Not because I don't think I could beat them on product and service, but because I don't have pockets as deep as theirs to weather a price cut for as long."

"Then you don't have anything to worry about." Earl sipped more coffee. "Just because they're bigger doesn't mean they don't want to make a profit. No one's in business to lose money. Hell, they might even raise the prices around here—you know, wait things out with that financial backing you mentioned, take a few losses while they figure out what the local market could handle. Keene'd be free to do the same—to raise its prices, too. Everyone would come out ahead."

"Or they might not mind losing some profit up front to clean up big in the end." She stared out the window at the sudden clamor of a couple of gulls dueling over the pastry crumbs Crazy Ed had tossed on the dock. "Continental doesn't want any competition at all, and once they've moved into an area, they've managed to get rid of it. That's their usual pattern."

She turned her cup in tight circles on the table. "All they'd have to do is lower the local prices below what we could afford to compete with. It wouldn't take long for them to bleed Keene dry. And they'd end up with it all."

"You can't be sure that's what would happen." Earl dismissed her worries with a shrug. "Besides, that's no concern of mine. Sorry, but that's the way it is."

Charlie acknowledged his admission with a short, tense nod. "I know that, Earl. But you can see where that leaves Keene Concrete—in competition with you, just like always. I guarantee you, there'll be a race to see which one of us sells and which one gets left behind to deal with Continental. And believe me, with a buyer's market like that, the selling price is going to head south fast."

"No one's going to have to sell at a loss," he said. But Charlie saw the hint of panic behind the calculation in his eyes.

"I'd prefer not to have to sell at all," she said. "But now that Continental's in town, it'll probably pick up one of our outfits for a song. And be in a stronger position to drive the other one into the ground."

Earl's face flushed a deep red. "If David had kept his nose out of all this, there wouldn't be any competition for a sale."

"David's been wanting to sell ever since our father died. You know that."

"But you still don't want to."

"No, I don't."

"What about Maudie?"

Charlie picked up her coffee and sipped, hoping her expression wouldn't give him a clue about her gut-twisting fear. "What about her?"

"What does she think about all this?"

"She's not real happy about Continental being here, either." It wasn't the answer Earl had wanted, but it was the only one he was going to get.

"So," he said, "what are you going to do about all this?"

"Nothing I wasn't going to do before." Charlie set down her coffee and folded her arms on the table. "Let me buy you out, Earl. You'll get the price you want for BayRock, and I'll get the deal I want for Keene. And we'll both keep Continental out of Carnelian Cove."

He waited until the waitress had set their breakfasts before them and freshened their coffees. "Sounds like it's time to stop dragging your feet on the financing, then," he said. "I want this settled, one way or the other. Before Continental settles it for me."

"You got it." She drizzled syrup over her pancakes and began slicing them into bite-size pieces. He'd managed to cover his unease with a layer of bluster, but she knew she'd finally driven the point of her argument through his thick, greedy skull. "And I want your promise you'll give me twenty-four hours' notice before you strike any kind of a deal with Continental."

He stared at her with a frown and then shrugged and tucked into his omelet. "All right."

"Selling out to Keene's the only solution. For you, for me, for the contractors here in Carnelian Cove. And you know I'll do my best to offer you a fairer price than Continental would."

She forked up a dripping piece of pancake and gave him a meaningful look. "Considering the circumstances."

CHAPTER ELEVEN

AFTER A BREAKFAST of blueberry pancakes—one of Jack's favorites—served with Agatha's update on the feud between the owners of the Organic Café and the diner down the road, he climbed the stairs to his Venetian sanctuary and checked his BlackBerry for messages. Two: the first hinting at cataclysmic developments in the San Francisco office, the second forecasting the destruction of life as he'd known it—both from Sally, his assistant. He shoved the bed pillows in an untidy heap against the four-poster's headboard and settled against them before punching her number. "Good mornin', Miss Sally."

"Jack."

"And what a fine morning it is, even for a Monday."

"That's what you think." She paused for a slurpy sip of the coffee she drank by the gallon. "You'd better get back down here. Pronto."

"What's up?"

"Noah. To no good."

Noah Fuller, a nemesis in the classic tradition. Every job came with built-in competition, and Noah appeared to have decided Jack was the man to beat—especially for the next opening in management. The current round of buyout rumors had merely upped the stakes.

Jack shifted on the bed with a sigh. "Not this again."

"I'm telling you, Jack, one of these days you'll thank me for looking out for your interests back at the office while you're traipsing through the countryside, yakking with the local yokels."

"Yakking with the locals is how I get the job done," said Jack.

"And you do it so well."

"The job?"

"The yakking."

He smiled. Sally would never admit it, but she could be quite the talker, too, when it suited her purposes. That's one of the reasons he'd taken her on as part of the team.

"Listen up," she said. "Lucy in Marketing told Paul in Human Resources that she overheard Noah discussing an Oregon supply source with Mullens."

"Oregon's too far away," said Jack. "Shipping would be too expensive. Besides, Mullens doesn't work on the supply end. Noah's barking up the wrong tree."

"But Mullens plays racquetball with Hanrahan every Wednesday at the gym. And Hanrahan is—"

"Hanrahan is Peterson's right-hand man." And Peterson was on the team that made the final decisions on the top management spots. Noah might be up to something, all right. And whether that something was a lead on an Oregon gravel source or an in with the big dogs, Jack should probably muster the enthusiasm to check into it.

He crossed his legs and gazed out the window at the San

Marcos suite's view of the Carnelian Cove waterfront. A fishing boat made a late-start sprint out of the bay, and his new friend Ed sat on the dock tossing doughnut crumbs to swooping, argumentative gulls. The only thing he could muster up some enthusiasm for at the moment was finding out the location of the baker that had supplied that doughnut and checking out whether those doughnuts were fresh. And glazed.

"*Jack.*"

"I'm here." He dragged his gaze from the window. "Been thinking."

"About getting on a plane and heading back in time to meet with Bill this afternoon, I hope."

"I don't have a meeting scheduled."

"Want me to get you one?"

"Nothing definite to report yet. So," he said, shifting into a more comfortable position, "there's no point in hopping on that plane."

"You keep forgetting Noah's down here, looking for a nice, dull knife to stab into your back."

Sally had her own reasons for keeping an eye on Noah. She knew that if Jack got a promotion, he'd take her with him. While he'd hired her for her agile mind and cool efficiency, her ambition had been a bonus. Most people thought the world ran on oil and the like, but Jack figured the real fuel was incentive.

"Speaking of unpleasant things," he said, "what have you heard about Moore's offer for Continental?"

It wasn't often that Sally let such a long pause fall into

a conversation, particularly one involving business. Jack frowned. "That bad, huh?"

"One of the reasons I want you to come back is to keep Bill from jumping out his office window."

"Moore would be crazy to let Bill go."

"You know how it is," said Sally. "The more expensive guys at the top are the first to get lost in the takeover shuffle."

Business. Sometimes it just didn't pay to be the best at what you did. "Maybe good news from Carnelian Cove will give a Bill a few more bargaining chips," he said.

"And maybe Noah will be able to make his case that your latest long-shot fishing expedition isn't worth the effort and expense, considering, and I quote, 'the recent signs of a possible downturn in the market and the continuing economic instability in the region.'"

"Bull. Shit."

"Succinct," said Sally after another sip of her coffee, "but too colorful for an interoffice e-mail. What do— Excuse me."

Jack ran a hand through his hair, waiting on hold. Corporate intrigue was a bigger waste of effort and money than anything else he could imagine. Locating and securing new sources of building materials was essential for a fast-growing company like Continental. And it would be equally essential to Moore Enterprises, if that larger company bought Jack's employer.

Things didn't get more basic than sand and gravel—the stuff was in every road, bridge and building foundation in the country. Gravel lined country roads and railroad tracks; sand was part of the glue bonding bricks together. A construction company without access to a steady supply of either material would stumble to a halt at the first stage of any job.

Guys like Noah—who'd never spent a day roofing in hundred-degree heat, who'd never guided a backhoe down a muddy slope in a rainstorm, who'd never welded copper pipe or pulled wire or hung drywall—would never understand what it took to pull a project together. Getting out of the office helped Jack stay in touch with the basics beneath the corporate deals. Places like Carnelian Cove reminded him where he'd come from. And, he realized as he stared out Agatha's window, got him thinking about where he'd like to end up.

He reached behind his head and bunched the pillows. He'd have to touch base with Bill later in the day and discuss the basics. He'd remind Bill why it had been such a good idea to head north and check out the possibilities in Carnelian Cove—just as soon as he got a better grip on himself. Ever since his dinner date with Charlie, things seemed to be unraveling at the edges.

"Jack."

"Still here."

"Well, it's been fun," said Sally, "but I'd better go stomp out another brushfire before it flares up and destroys the west coast office. My boss is funny about things like that."

She disconnected, and he dropped the BlackBerry on the rumpled quilt. Sally was right—he should kick up his pace here so he could scurry on home to keep an eye on Noah. And Bill. And Mullens, Hanrahan and Peterson. He should get a firmer grip on that corporate ladder, in case

Moore Enterprises grabbed hold and gave the thing a hard shake.

He stared at the hems of his jeans and waited for his ambition to kick in, for the killer instinct to drive him out the door and into the fray. And then a channel buoy clanged, and he glanced outside to see Ed fasten a pinch of pastry on his hook and drop his line in the water.

Carnelian Cove was proving to be a surprising distraction. He hadn't thought a place could tug at him in quite this way, but the combination of interesting scenery and intriguing inhabitants was casting a strange spell. San Francisco seemed a world away instead of a couple of hundred miles down the coast, and the competitive urgency that drove him so hard when he was in the city seemed to dissipate each morning when the fog cleared.

He glanced at his watch. He figured he had just enough time before his morning appointment to discover the source of those doughnuts and share a couple with Ed. And then, to fill his afternoon with some productive activity, he could check on Charlie Keene. Just for the hell of it.

A smile spread across his face, and he swung his legs over the edge of the bed and planted his slightly scruffy sports shoes on the floor. Tracking down Charlie seemed the best incentive yet for getting a start on the business day.

JACK GUIDED HIS CAR AROUND another curve in the narrow road that climbed the heights at the north end of town, and then he slowed with a soft whistle. "Geneva Chandler," he said as he stared at a shingled mansion crowding the edge of a bluff, "you must be one hell of a rich old lady."

Wealthier than Agatha had estimated, he thought as he entered an expansive estate through a tall black iron gate. Classier than the bakery-shop clerk had suggested, if the elegant, neatly trimmed landscaping was any indication. And wilier than an old fox with a yen for the fattest hen in the coop, if his snooping had managed to turn up the truth.

He knew why he was here—to meet the town matriarch and try to get a feel for how many strings she might be pulling behind the scenes. He wondered how long it would take him to figure out what Geneva planned to gain with her request for this meeting.

He slowed again as he passed beneath a porte cochere and stopped at the base of the wide stone steps leading to the leaded-glass entry. Ivy trailed from concrete urns planted with boxwood and dotted with primroses, and hairy frond curls rose from the hearts of sleeping ferns. By midsummer, the twisting wisteria canes and naked climbing roses would bloom with a colorful welcome to Chandler House.

Now that the fog had cleared, late-morning light glinted in faceted glass as the massive front door swung wide to reveal the acknowledged queen of Carnelian Cove. Tall and trim, dressed in tailored wool and diamond-trimmed pearls, Geneva stepped onto the porch amid a flood of yipping Yorkies. The soft waves of her white hair, gathered in a twist at the back of her head, framed the kind of long, angular face that was photogenic in youth and delicate in later years. The kind of face that could frost over a smile or heat up a frown.

Jack ordered himself not to fidget with his tie as he

climbed the steps. "Good morning, Mrs. Chandler. I'm Jack Maguire."

"Hello, Mr. Maguire. Welcome to Chandler House." She extended a hand to take his in a surprisingly firm grip. "I hope you didn't have any trouble finding your way here."

"No, ma'am." Jack gave her one of his most disarming smiles, the one he used to loosen up the stiffest social occasions. "Your directions were perfect."

"Practice makes them that way." She led him into a high-ceilinged foyer lit by a chandelier dripping with crystal.

His heels clicked on the black-and-white marble floor. "I imagine so."

"Do you?" She paused and leveled her clear blue eyes on his. "What else do you imagine?"

"About you?"

"If I'm to be the subject of this conversation."

He smiled and shoved his hands into his pockets. "That would be a pleasant way to spend the morning."

"Rather than being grilled about yourself?"

He tilted his head to one side. "If that's to be the method of this conversation."

"I'd heard you were a likable young man." Geneva's lips twitched. "But I didn't plan on liking you myself."

"Life can be a great deal more interesting when our plans change in unexpected ways, don't you think, Mrs. Chandler?"

"I think you may be right, Mr. Maguire."

"Do you think you might decide to call me Jack?"

"Perhaps."

She turned and continued through tall pocket doors into

a darkly papered parlor furnished with antiques and scented with the lilies crowding a tall crystal vase.

Jack studied the portrait hanging above the fireplace mantel. "Is this a relative?"

"My late husband."

"Handsome man."

"Yes. Yes, he was. Before his drinking aged him prematurely and then took its own sweet time killing him."

Jack wondered whether he should offer an expression of sympathy but then decided she didn't need that from anyone. Especially from a stranger.

She gestured toward one of the chairs arranged in a windowed alcove, and he waited for her to settle in another before taking his seat. "Tea?" she asked as she lifted a rose-covered pot from the silver tray at her side. "Or lemonade?"

"Tea, thank you."

"You don't strike me as the tea type." She poured a cup and tucked a slice of shortbread on his saucer before passing it to him. "Any more than you strike me as the type to do the kind of work you do."

"What kind of work do you think I should do?" he asked.

"I'll answer that question later." She sipped her tea and leaned back. "Once we understand each other better."

"Does anyone around these parts really understand you, Mrs. Chandler?"

She gave him a long, hard stare. "I do believe it's time for you to call me Geneva, Jack."

"All right. Geneva it is." He bit into his shortbread. "What is it you want me to understand?"

"I'm a good customer of Keene Concrete as well as a

friend of the family." She took another sip of tea. "I have a large construction project currently in development, and I don't want the financing affected or the material delivery schedules disrupted."

"There's no reason for either of those things to happen."

"Even if Continental changes hands?"

He shouldn't have been surprised Geneva had heard the rumors—he figured there wasn't much the woman didn't know about anything affecting her business or personal interests. Now he wondered what Charlie had heard—and why, if she knew anything about the situation, she hadn't mentioned it.

He gazed at Geneva over the gold rim of his cup. "Even so."

"Business as usual?"

"Especially at a time like this."

"And is it usual for Continental to look so far afield? So far from larger markets?"

"It's not the market that's the attraction." He hesitated, wondering how much he could—or should—say. How much she already knew. A woman like Geneva would have a network of sources beyond Carnelian Cove. "I'm here to assess other possibilities."

"I understand you've met with Earl Sawyer to discuss BayRock's sale."

"That's partially right, at any rate. I have met with him."

"I can imagine the possibilities you discussed. What I can't imagine is why BayRock. And why now."

"It's simple enough," said Jack. "Supply and demand."

"The city's demand. Our supply."

"It's a possibility." Jack lowered his cup to its saucer. "I'd ask what else you imagined—or weren't able to imagine—about my discussion with Earl, but I wouldn't want to appear to be grilling my hostess."

"Are you suggesting I'm interrogating you, Jack?"

"Not answering that question would be just about as impolite as answering in the affirmative or lying."

His hostess's lips quivered as she struggled to suppress a smile. "That's no answer."

"Then I beg your pardon."

They sipped their tea in silence. Jack took a moment to appreciate the view—the sweep of emerald lawn, the black gash of scarred rock, the dramatic rise of tall trees, the rippling gray-green of the ocean.

"What do you think of Carnelian Cove?" Geneva asked.

"It's a pleasant enough town." He grinned. "With some interesting people."

"Interesting?"

"Yes, ma'am."

"Again, Jack, that's no real answer."

"I'd heard it was a likable town," he said as his grin widened. "But I didn't plan on liking it myself."

"No, I don't suppose you did." Her gaze sharpened. "It's not the city."

He shook his head. "No, ma'am, it's not. But then, San Francisco is one of a kind."

"You'd miss it. If you left."

He set his cup and saucer aside and sank more comfortably in his chair, enjoying the twists and turns of Geneva's conversation. "And just why would I leave?"

"You've made a habit of leaving, of moving from one place to the next."

When he didn't respond, she set her own cup and saucer aside. "I doubt that your information about me," she said, "is any less thorough than mine about you."

"Which makes me wonder why you extended the invitation for this visit."

He waited patiently while Geneva lifted the teapot from the tray. She offered him more tea and shortbread, which he refused.

"I wanted to judge for myself what kind of man you are," she said at last as she settled back against her chair. "And now that I know, I'm going to answer your question about the kind of work I think you should do."

She crossed her legs and straightened a pleat on her skirt. "I think you should be doing something for yourself, Jack."

He gave her a carefully neutral smile. "I do just fine for myself with the work I do."

"I'm not talking about financial compensation. I'm talking about working for yourself. Making your own opportunities. Taking charge of your future."

His gut tightened with a familiar ache—the ambition that had gone missing this morning. "Owning my own business."

"Yes." She nodded slowly. "I can see the idea is one you've considered before."

"I s'pose every employee has considered the idea at some point or other."

"But not in San Francisco, unique as it is."

"No." He liked the city well enough and had enjoyed his time there, but it wasn't home. Not the vague idea he had of what home should be, at any rate.

Geneva tapped a slender finger on the arm of her chair. "Maudie Keene is a good friend of mine."

And, Jack figured, the true reason behind this invitation to tea. "Charlie's mother."

"And David's." Geneva arched an eyebrow. "You met with David, I heard."

"He showed me around the Keene operation. And Charlie joined me for dinner the other night." He forced himself to relax. "I'm sure you've heard about that, too."

"An interesting young woman."

"That she is."

"A difficult young woman."

He managed to keep his grin from spreading too wide. "I suspect she can be."

"You don't find her difficult?"

"Should I?"

Geneva's lips pressed together in a thin, foxlike smile. "Will you stay for lunch, Jack?"

CHAPTER TWELVE

MAUDIE OPENED HER DOOR shortly after dinner on Monday evening to find Ben on her front porch. "Ben! What a nice surprise."

He smiled shyly and extended a huge bouquet of white iris and baby blush tulips. "I hope you don't mind my stopping by without calling first."

"No, not at all. Please, come in—it's freezing out there." She took the flowers and headed toward the kitchen. "These are beautiful," she called over her shoulder. "You spoil me so."

"I enjoy spoiling you." He hesitated near the counter, watching her arrange the flowers in a vase. "I hope you'll let me keep spoiling you for a long, long time."

She paused, as her breath caught in her throat and her stomach filled with lead, and stared at him. "Just how long did you have in mind, Ben?"

He moved into the room and took both her hands in his. "Forever, if you'll have me."

"Are you asking me to marry you?"

"Yes, Maudie. I am."

"This is a surprise, too." And oh, no, it shouldn't have been. She'd been too swept up in the emotion—and the unexpected passion—of the day before to look ahead to this moment. She should have known Ben would look ahead. With expectations.

Ben. Oh, Ben. Slowly, carefully, she freed her hands from his.

"It shouldn't be such a big surprise," he said, his smile fading. "Not after yesterday afternoon."

She sank into a chair at her kitchen table and carefully ran her fingers over the linen. "Yesterday afternoon was very precious to me."

"And to me." He took the chair facing hers. "I didn't want you to think I planned to take advantage of…the situation."

She gave him a level look. "A marriage proposal is a rather extreme method of apologizing, don't you think?"

"I'm not apologizing." He reddened and shifted in his seat. "Although I suppose I should, for the way I'm going about this."

"Ben." She shoved her hands through her hair and then dropped them into her lap. The awkward moments had given her time to recover, although she was still struggling for the right words, for some perfect phrase to get them through the awkward moments to come. "One of the reasons yesterday meant so much to me is that you helped me feel things I hadn't felt in years. I'm not talking about the things we did in bed, though every moment of that was lovely. Truly lovely, and a memory I'll always treasure."

She worked up a smile for him, though she could feel the strain at the edges and knew he could see the effort, too. "I'm talking about the things you said before that, in this room."

"I meant every word."

"I'm sure you did." Staring at her hands, she laced her fingers together and squeezed until the knuckles turned white. "You've always been completely honest with me."

"I always will be, Maudie."

"I know that." She lifted her gaze to his. "It's one of the things I love about you."

"Damn." He sat back and blew out a disgusted sigh. "There it is. The *L* word."

She sputtered through a laugh, and a great deal of her tension drifted away. "Did you think I wouldn't notice you hadn't mentioned it yet?"

"I've really mangled things tonight." He glanced at her with a boyish grin. "I don't suppose you'd let me step out on your front porch and start over?"

She shook her head. A familiar pressure was building inside her chest. "I don't want to have to fuss with the flowers again."

"Maudie, I—"

"Wait." She took a shaky breath. "I started to say that yesterday you helped find something buried deep inside me. Something I thought I'd lost. And for a few minutes, I felt young again. And stronger than I've felt in a long, long time."

He reached across the table, his palm up, and waited until she slipped her hand into his. "Let me do that for you again."

"No, Ben." Her smile wasn't as wobbly as she'd feared it would be. "I can't let you do something I need to learn to do for myself."

He lowered his eyes to their hands as he closed his fingers around hers and squeezed. Long, painful moments passed, moments filled with the ticking of the hall clock and her irrational resentment that Mitch had died and left her behind to deal with this mess.

Ben cleared his throat. "I understand." He dragged his hand back across the linen, wrinkling the cloth. "Although I wish you'd reconsider your answer to my proposal. Even if it was one of the worst proposals ever."

"Perhaps I will. Someday." She smoothed the cloth and stood, giving him a falsely bright smile. "In the meantime, you can practice your technique."

"Good idea." He rose from his chair and hesitated, looking deflated and unsure of his next move.

For one terrifying moment, she was afraid she'd either burst into tears or nervous laughter at the sight of strong, straight Ben Chandler looking like someone had let the air out of his tires. And in the next, another irrational, extreme impulse took hold of her.

She stepped toward him and skimmed her fingers along the lapels of his suit. "Will you kiss me good-night?"

He wrapped his long arms around her waist and pulled her against him, so tightly she could hardly draw a breath. "I wasn't sure you'd want me to," he said.

She closed her eyes and let herself go, let herself bask in his warmth, in the pleasure and security of a solid form so much bigger and stronger than hers. But she wanted more. She wanted him.

She wiggled free to reach up and brush her lips across his. "You know," she murmured, "your proposals might need some practice, but there's nothing wrong with your lovemaking."

"Maudie." He buried his face in her hair. "I do love you."

"I thought that might be the case." She placed a row of teasing kisses along his jaw, smiling at the freshly shaved smoothness and the sharp scent of his cologne. "I was hoping you'd show me exactly how much."

She'd surprised him—she saw it in his frown as she took him by the hand and tugged him out of the kitchen and started toward her room. They'd both have to recover from the evening's surprises. She was eager to try, to move past the awkwardness and laugh with him again. Eager to learn more about what pleased him. "That's one thing I don't mind you doing for me," she said. "Making me feel loved. Making me feel *young*."

"What do you mean?" He stopped in the hallway. "Are you suggesting we sleep together?"

She bit back a smile at his mortified expression. "You didn't seem to mind climbing into bed with me yesterday afternoon."

"That was before—" He frowned. "I don't want to have an affair with you, Maudie."

"I'm not su—" But that's exactly what she was suggesting. If she took him as a lover but wouldn't agree to marry him, they'd be having an affair.

The idea was shocking, and she tensed and waited for it to shame her, to bring her to her senses. She stared at the tall, wide-shouldered man standing in her hall, waiting for her response—waiting for her to agree with him, to do what he wanted her to do—and her tension increased.

"Maudie?"

She didn't want to be tense anymore. She didn't want

to feel like she owed a man the answer he expected instead of the one she was willing to give. "I'll walk you to the door."

He swallowed. "If that's what you want."

"I'm not sure what I want at the moment," she said as she led the way to the front of the house. "But I know what I don't."

"My company," said Ben with a sad smile.

She grabbed his jacket lapels and tugged him down to brush a kiss across his lips. "I adore your company. But I need some time for myself tonight."

She closed the door behind him and leaned against it with a long, shaky sigh. Getting back in touch with the old, hell-raising Maudie was going to be hell on the new one.

JACK STOOD ON CHARLIE'S ramshackle front porch Monday night, frowning at the spindly weeds in her fat barrel planter and the faded stain on the siding. The house had potential— a classic design and a roomy yard, tucked beneath mature trees in a comfortable neighborhood—but it looked sadly neglected. If it were his, he'd take a great deal of pleasure in plans for improvements and the sweat to make them happen. He'd make a start by sanding down this solid old door, adding a fresh coat of paint and a black iron knocker, maybe one of those pieces he'd seen at that blacksmith's shop.

It was a lot easier to consider something as basic as repairs than the reason he was standing here contemplating them. Easier to cruise along in a mindless fashion, heading in Charlie's general direction while remaining in a state of denial.

But the fact remained that he'd spent a great deal of time today searching for an excuse—any excuse—to spend some private time with her.

And he'd arrived bearing flowers and candy.

Damn. How could he explain that to either of them? He stared at the things in his hands. This didn't look good. No, from where he was standing—clutching his ridiculous gifts and wanting nothing so much as another opportunity to look at Charlie, and talk to her, and touch her—this didn't look good at all.

Where was a dose of denial when a fellow needed it?

Before he could knock—or make his escape—the hound from hell sounded the alarm. A few moments later, the door opened an inch or so and Charlie and her black beast peered through the narrow opening.

"Evenin', Charlie."

She frowned and struggled to keep Hardy from shoving through. "What are you doing here?"

"I stopped by the store to pick up some caramel squares. I sure am partial to caramel squares," he added. "Especially on a long drive. Or during a movie, if my conscience can tolerate smuggling them into the theater. The prices some movie houses charge for popcorn and candy is more than the price of the ticket these days. And the selection isn't all that good, especially for caramels."

He knew he was rambling, but it was so much fun watching her expression shift from suspicion to annoyance, with that momentary detour to confusion along the way. Her eyebrows lowered in a frown above her freckled nose, and he itched to skim a finger over the creases between them.

Hardy whined and strained against his collar, and she tugged him back. "What does the price of a theater ticket have to do with you standing on my doorstep?"

"Not as much as it has to do with the difficulty of finding a good caramel for the price of admission. I'll settle for Milk Duds, when I have to, but I'm mostly a purist when it comes to caramels. I prefer mine without chocolate."

She rolled her eyes toward the ceiling, just as he'd known she would. "Thank you for stopping by to explain. I'll do my best to avoid offering you chocolate-covered caramel."

"I'd appreciate it." He smiled and shifted the items in his arms, extending a box of seedlings. "These are for you."

"Why?" She tightened her grip on the panting dog's collar as she reached through the door to take the box.

"They were spread out on a display table near the aisle with the caramels. I thought they'd brighten up your front porch a bit. Maybe you could plant them here, in this old barrel."

"Thank you." She stared at the seedlings.

"They're primroses," he said.

"Yes, I—I can see that."

She glanced up at him, and the expression on her face squeezed at his chest so hard he had difficulty drawing his next breath. "What's the matter?" he asked. "Don't you like primroses?"

"No. I mean, I do. I— Never mind." She nudged Hardy aside with her knee and opened the door wider. "Come in."

"Thank you for the invitation." He rubbed his hand over the dog's head as he stepped in, trying to disguise his efforts to keep the animal down and his paws off his jacket. "I hope I'm not disturbing your supper."

"Finished." Obviously flustered, she set the flowers on a deep windowsill and lifted an overflowing laundry basket from her ugly brown sofa. "Have a seat."

He settled on one side and was immediately involved in a shoving match when Hardy tried to climb into his lap. "Someone should explain the basic rules of acceptable dog behavior to this animal."

"Be my guest."

He turned his most dazzling smile on her. "I was hoping you'd make that offer tonight."

She rolled her eyes again and carried the laundry down a narrow hall—toward her bedroom, he figured. He wondered if her room was furnished with more of the mismatched, threadbare items she'd scattered about her front room. Some of the pieces had potential—that claw-footed chair in the corner, for instance. Some sanding, a fresh coat of varnish, perhaps a throw to hide the stained upholstery until it could be replaced.

Hardy sniffed and nudged at the brown bag dangling from Jack's fingers as Charlie wandered back into the room. "Let me guess," she said, nodding at the package. "Caramel squares."

"Among other things. I wasn't sure what kind of candy you like to snack on while you watch a movie, so I brought an assortment."

"We're watching a movie?"

"We could," he said as he leaned back. "If you've got one to watch. I prefer shoot-'em-up films, but I can tolerate a drama if the actresses are pretty and don't tear up too often." He patted the cushion beside him. "Or we could sit and have ourselves a nice visit. Caramels go well with conversation, too."

"I'm going to ask again," she said with a sigh, "although I'm beginning to think I won't get an answer before noon tomorrow. Why are you here?"

Good question. One deserving a decent answer. Maybe he'd manage to come up with that answer, for them both, by the end of the evening.

Before his mind turned to mush trying to puzzle it out, he caught her by the wrist and tugged her down beside him. "I stopped by for a visit," he said. "Just a friendly visit, though I s'pose we could talk business, if you'd prefer."

"We could have talked business on the phone."

He slid his fingers down the back of her hand. She smelled of her faintly fruity shampoo and diesel fuel—and the fact that he found the combination as intoxicating as the most expensive perfume amused and alarmed him. "If I'd called," he pointed out, "you wouldn't have those flowers for your planter."

"I don't need flowers."

"Maybe not, but they're nice to have around, don't you think?"

"I'm sorry. I didn't mean to sound ungrateful." She shifted to face him, putting a few inches between them at the same time. "They're very nice. Thank you."

"You're welcome, particularly as the pleasure's partly mine."

He brushed a hand through her curls, skimming his fingers along her warm, slender neck, and her tiny shiver made his mouth go dry. "A man enjoys bringing flowers to the woman in his life."

Her eyes fluttered closed when he cupped the back of her head and lowered his face toward hers. "You're not the man in my life," she said.

"I'm the man who's here."

"Why?" she whispered against his lips.

He brushed his mouth, light as a dandelion puff, over hers. Once, twice. A third time, just because she tasted nearly as good as caramel squares. "Because I've been thinking about kissing you." He slid an arm around her waist and pulled her closer. "And I don't like it."

"Kissing me?"

"Thinking about kissing you. Nearly every moment of the day."

She lifted her arms and pressed her hands against his chest, and he held his breath, wondering if she'd push him away. But then she curled her fingers into his shirt.

"Then don't," she whispered as she raised her face toward his.

"Think about it?"

"Kiss me."

"Yes, ma'am."

This—this simple, incredibly perfect contact—this was one reason he'd bought those simple bits of greenery and traveled the route leading to this place. He'd wanted to see her eyes go wide and dark when he touched her, wanted to hear that tiny hitch in her breath when he pulled her close. Wanted to rub his mouth over hers and swallow her soft sighs.

He nipped at her lower lip before sinking into a sweet, lingering caress, and then he guided her back, never losing contact with her soft, lush mouth, and followed her down, down, stretching over her and slipping one leg between hers. Her compact body was as comfortable and inviting as her sofa cushions.

"This isn't what I meant," she murmured against his mouth.

"It isn't?" He ran his tongue along her earlobe and smiled when she moaned. "Do you like that better?"

"Jack."

"Hmm?"

"I thought we'd agreed this wasn't a good idea."

"Not exactly." He lowered his forehead to hers and kissed the tip of her nose. "You're the one who said that."

"So what are you doing?"

"Trying to change your mind."

She laughed and wrapped an arm around his neck and kissed him again, playfully running her tongue around the edge of his lips, and it was his turn to shiver with pleasure. He plunged a hand beneath her sweatshirt and stroked his way up to the thin layer of her bra, brushing his thumb back and forth across the silky fabric as he sank against her.

A deep growl rumbled through the room. Jack froze.

"Hardy," she murmured against his mouth.

"I figured."

The growl grew louder.

"Don't make any sudden moves," she said.

"I won't, I promise."

She leaned to the side and scratched her bodyguard behind one ear. "Wazza matter, baby? Is mean ol' Jack boddering your mommy? What a good boy, what a good boy you are." She took him by the collar and dragged him toward the dining room. "I'll be right back."

Mean ol' Jack rolled his head against the back of the sofa and stared at her water-stained ceiling. As an exit cut, Hardy couldn't be beat.

He rose from his seat as she entered the room, intending to make a polite farewell. But there she stood, with her thick, tousled hair framing her flushed cheeks and her smoky eyes filled with a disturbing combination of desire and doubt, and his gut tightened as the answer he'd been seeking sucker punched him right beneath his ribs. With every aspect of his life in flux, the one constant was his craving for this woman.

No sense in asking why. The answer to that particular question didn't matter.

"Sorry about that," she said. "I guess you're going to leave now."

"I wondered how long it would take you to bring up your favorite subject."

"What's that?"

"My imminent departure."

She hesitated, pulling at the hem of her worn sweatshirt, and then she gave him a shy smile and stepped closer. "You're probably out of luck tonight. I'll bet the last flight to San Francisco already left."

"I could always hit the highway in my rental."

"Yes, you could." She took another step toward him.

"I've even got a bag of caramels to sustain me during the drive," he said.

"That's convenient.

"Are you staying?"

"We haven't watched the movie yet," he pointed out.

"Jack." She rolled her eyes. "There is no movie."

"Seems a shame to waste all this movie candy." He shrugged theatrically and headed toward the door. "And I didn't get a chance to tell you about my visit with Geneva Chandler."

"You met Geneva?"

"I had lunch with her." He grabbed the doorknob. "At her house."

"At her house?"

"That's right." He opened the door. "See you around."

"*Jack.*"

Charlie shoved her hands through her hair with an I-surrender sigh. "All right. You win. Here's the remote," she said, waving the plastic wand in the air. "I'm sure you'll find something with plenty of shoot-'em-up stuff on cable."

"And explosions." He took the remote, settled back against the soft cushions and stacked his feet on the sorry-looking trunk that passed for her coffee table. "A car chase or two would be nice, too."

Charlie snatched the bag from him. "Got any chocolate?"

He nodded, pleased with the trace of a smile on her face and his decision to stay. "Dark and light."

"Good," she said as she headed toward her back door and her howling dog. "I need a double."

CHAPTER THIRTEEN

JACK RELAXED AT THE CORNER table of Mona's, a coffee shop near the marina in Carnelian Cove's old town district, reading the want ads in the Tuesday-morning edition of *The Cove Press*. College students and young executives sipped organic beverages from hand-painted mugs and crunched homemade biscotti. Mona herself worked the counter, dispensing fair-trade lattes and cappuccinos with a sprinkle of cinnamon and the occasional reminder about an upcoming peace rally.

Earl Sawyer entered the shop and paused near the door, staring with disgust at a row of paintings spoofing da Vinci's smiling lady in various settings and violent shades. He shook his head as he stalked down the aisle to join Jack at his table. "Waste of paint."

"I don't know about that." Jack folded the paper and set it aside. "I sort of liked *Deep Sea Mona*."

"Was that the one where she's got a goldfish bowl over her head?"

"No, that was *Mona Under Glass*."

Sawyer scowled at a young woman in dreadlocks and a Che T-shirt as she passed their table.

"Can I buy you a cup of coffee?" asked Jack.

"As long as it's not that foamy stuff." Sawyer squinted at the selections on a chalkboard tacked to the brick wall. "Don't they have any plain old coffee?"

"You could try the Kona roast."

"Kona?" asked Sawyer suspiciously. "Is it from Hawaii?"

"That's my theory." Jack paid for two coffees, two gigantic cinnamon rolls and a glazed doughnut to go for Ed and carried them back to the table. His choice of location for this meeting may have been a touch extreme. But it was one place he'd been fairly certain their conversation wouldn't be interrupted by friends or acquaintances of Sawyer's stopping by to say hello. And knocking his opponent off balance before he landed his first combination one-two punch was Jack's usual business tactic.

Although he sure didn't feel like doing business in the usual manner this morning. He'd enjoyed his stroll down the hill from the bed and breakfast. The wind had whisked away the fog early this morning and whipped up tiny white caps on the bay. He'd stopped by that blacksmith's shop again and admired a countertop wine rack he thought he might buy for Agatha before he left. And he'd discovered Addie's stained-glass window shop and stepped inside for a visit. Her designs were as beautiful as their creator, every bit as whimsical and delicate.

Sawyer sampled his coffee and leaned back with a nod. "Not bad."

Jack smiled. "Sorry to drag you all the way down here, but Agatha recommended it."

"Figured as much." Sawyer stared at Jack over the rim of his mug. "So, what's up?"

"I got to wondering about a couple of things." Jack twisted his coffee in a slow circle on the table. "I'm wondering how you might feel about a little competition—a competing bid—once you get ready to sell your business."

"Don't mind that kind of competition at all. And I'm ready to sell. Right now, this week." Sawyer lowered his mug to the table. "The only reason I haven't sold it yet is because the one party that was interested has been dragging her feet for weeks on the financing."

"Financing can be tricky." Jack sat back with a sympathetic sigh. "Banks tend to want plenty of documentation for those sizable loans. Appraisals, profit and loss statements, that sort of thing."

"I've got everything that's needed, all filled out and ready to go. I'll gladly hand the copies over to anyone who wants to take a look." Sawyer squinted again, but this time it was calculation and not the decor that had sharpened his expression. "Like I said, I don't mind a little competition."

"No, I guess you wouldn't, seeing as how a little competition's all it takes to make what they call a seller's market."

Sawyer shrugged nonchalantly. "Supply and demand."

"Supply and demand." Jack nodded in agreement. He stretched his legs into the aisle, crossing his ankles in a casual pose. He'd been through a dozen negotiations like this, with a dozen calculating sellers just like Sawyer who thought they could make a sizable profit from a shift in circumstances.

Normally he relished this point in the discussion, but today he wasn't feeling the usual enthusiasm for what came next. Today he genuinely liked the fellow across the table—and the other players in the game—and it sapped some of the enjoyment from the job. Today his gaze kept returning to the view out the window and the crazy artwork on the walls. And his thoughts kept drifting to his meeting with Geneva.

And those caramel-flavored kisses of the night before.

"Supply and demand," said Jack, dragging his thoughts back with an effort. "That's a key concept to keep in mind, all right. The thing is, the market around here's only going to have one, maybe two interested parties. There's not much going on in this part of the state."

"There's enough here to keep two outfits going."

"It'd be better with one."

Sawyer frowned. "One outfit?"

Jack nodded. "Seems to me that's what Keene is trying to pull off, buying you out. Makes a whole lot of sense. Sometimes having no competition's the best way to survive in a small market like this one."

Two young women squeezed past, and Sawyer eyed their tattoos with a mix of curiosity and disapproval. "I don't know what that has to do with anything. Keene Concrete isn't for sale," he said.

"Anything's for sale, at the right price." Jack straightened and tucked his legs beneath his chair. "You're closing up shop, and Keene's interested. If I were a guy who was also interested in getting a piece of the business up this way, I might think things would work out more to my advantage to wait for Keene to snap up your operation for me. For one thing, it would probably save me the trouble of dealing with all that tricky documentation twice."

Sawyer's face was a touch flushed around the edges, but he was holding his tongue so far. Jack had to give him credit for keeping his emotions in check. It was never easy to sit and listen to a man blast a gaping hole in your hopes—especially when it was the same man who'd inflated them in the first place.

"Seems to me," Jack continued, "the smart thing to do would be to see if there's a way to work things around so that it's a buyer's market."

Sawyer stared at his cooling coffee for a moment and then shook his head with a short laugh. "Charlie was right."

"About what?"

"About all of this."

Sawyer rose, pulled his wallet out of his back pocket and tossed a couple of crumpled bills on the table. "She's a hell of a lot more competition for you than you think," he said. "I have a feeling that'll be my one consolation—watching that little girl give you the biggest fight you've ever had."

CHARLIE WAS IN A FOUL MOOD when she steered her pickup into the yard at Keene Concrete shortly before lunch on Tuesday, and seeing her mother's car parked in David's spot only added to the stink. She'd wasted an entire morning begging for help from her accountant and leniency from the loan officer at the bank, and she didn't have any patience to spare for her relatives at the moment.

She stalked into the office and shot a dark glance at Gus. "Where is she?"

"In David's office."

"With David?"

"Nope." Gus slurped his coffee. "He said something about some vacation time and took off before she got here."

Charlie ducked into her own office and swallowed a couple of pain relievers before heading down the hall. David's door was open, and her mother was watering the potted plant with one of the foam cups from the reception counter. Sunlight picked out the silver in her hair and glinted in the gold knots clipped to her ears. She straightened and turned with a slightly guilty look when Charlie entered.

"Mom." Charlie shoved her hands into her jeans pockets. "This is a surprise."

"For me, too." Maudie paused a moment and then dropped the cup in a waste bin and settled into David's desk chair. "Please, shut the door and have a seat. I'd like to talk to you."

Charlie turned to shut the door and froze. Her mother had decided to sell. Why else would she be here, sitting in David's spot, looking so businesslike and wearing one of the dressy suits she usually saved for church? "Where's David?" she asked.

"I don't know." Maudie sighed. "And I got the feeling when I asked Gus that same question this isn't the first time he's pulled this stunt."

Charlie slowly, quietly closed the door and carefully lowered herself into one of the visitors' chairs. She felt as if she were acting in a slow-motion movie. Time had warped; nothing was real. "Why does it matter?"

"Why does it—because it *should*. I'm surprised by your

attitude." Maudie blushed and clasped her hands on the desk. "Listen to me. I've been here all of one hour, and already I sound as if I'm taking charge. I'm afraid I'm not making a very good case for myself."

"A case?" This concern about David's whereabouts didn't sound like the beginning of the end, and Charlie began to relax. "What are you talking about?"

"The reason for this visit." Maudie squeezed her hands until her knuckles whitened and cleared her throat. "I've come to apply for a job."

"A job?"

"Yes. A job. I'm sure there must be something I can do to help out here. Perhaps I could start as David's assistant."

Charlie didn't want to disillusion Maudie about her son's contributions to the family business. "I'm not exactly sure how we'd go about training you to handle that position."

"Assistant bookkeeper, then. I may be a little out of practice—I'll admit that up front—but I'm very good with numbers."

"I'm sure you are." Charlie shook her head in amazement. "I just don't understand why you're here."

"I told you. I'd like a job." Maudie rubbed her fingers across the desktop as if she were scrubbing at a smudge. "Part-time would probably be best, for a while, until I'm used to the routine."

"Why here? Why now?"

"Where else should I look?" Maudie stood and paced to the window, her arms folded at her waist. "Isn't it the best strategy to start a job search where you have contacts?"

"Yes, but—"

"I know this comes as somewhat of a surprise, but it shouldn't. Not really. I've been working outside the home for years. My volunteer duties may not pay a salary, but I show up and I do what I'm asked. I can type up a résumé for you, if you need one."

Charlie shifted in her seat, uncomfortable with the thought of asking her mother for references—not to mention asking for her social security number. "I'm sure that won't be necessary. Considering that you're one of the owners."

"Yes, there is that," said Maudie with a tight smile. "Although I was hoping it wouldn't be too large a factor in your decision."

"It's kind of hard to ignore."

"So you have something for me to do?"

Charlie couldn't help but notice the hopeful tone in her mother's voice and the surprising assertiveness in her posture. It was indeed a shock seeing her here, seeing her like this, but Charlie hoped she'd be seeing a lot more of her mother looking exactly the way she did at this moment.

She put her hands on the chair arms and shoved to her feet. "I'm sure we can find something."

"Good." Maudie blew out a breath, and one of her hands fluttered to her stomach. "Do you want me to start today?"

"How about tomorrow?"

"Wednesday mornings I volunteer at the museum. I hope that won't be a problem until—"

"Don't worry about it." Charlie waved her concerns

away. "We can work around your schedule. And part-time sounds fine for now."

"I wouldn't want to take advantage. Of being an owner, I mean." Maudie smoothed her hand over her skirt. "How about afternoons?"

"Sounds great." Charlie stepped toward the door and then paused, turning to face her mother. "I still don't understand why you decided to come in today. You never mentioned you were considering this."

"I wasn't. Not until…recently. Very recently." Maudie blushed and straightened, lifting her chin. "It's time, I think. Time to move on and do something more with my life than sitting at home and being a widow."

That blush momentarily smothered Charlie's curiosity about her mother's motives. She really didn't want to know the details about what was making Maudie's cheeks so pink. But there was another issue that still troubled her. "I thought— When I first came in and saw you here, I thought you'd come to tell me you'd decided to sell. To Continental."

"I'd never do that."

Now it was Charlie's turn to release a pent-up sigh of relief. "Really?"

"I'm sorry I've let you think that was a possibility." Maudie sank into the desk chair. "I didn't want to disappoint either of my children."

"I never realized—" Charlie shook her head. "I'm sorry we've put you in such a tough situation."

"It goes with the territory." Maudie flashed a bright smile. "There's one more item for my résumé, to prove I can handle just about any job. Motherhood."

CHARLIE LOCKED THE GATE at Keene Concrete as the evening fog rolled in to obscure the stars and spread the bay's briny tang like a marinade over the river bar. She headed for her idling truck, pulled her cell phone from her pocket and punched in one of the numbers she had on speed dial. "Hey, Tess."

"Hey, yourself. Guess what I'm doing right now?"

"Picking up our pizza order?" Tess had bribed Charlie with one of Nino's sausage and mushroom specials to help plan a surprise birthday party for Addie. Their friend had uncovered the party plot two days after it had been hatched, but though the surprise was off, the party was still on.

"Already taken care of," said Tess.

Charlie climbed into her truck. "Starting dinner without me?"

"Because you're late again?" Hardy's excited barking nearly drowned Tess out. "Not that I'm nagging."

Charlie pulled onto the highway, heading toward town. "No, never that."

"You haven't guessed yet." Tess waited a beat. "I'll give you a hint. It involves Hottie Maguire and the black monster."

"Maguire's at my house again?" Charlie pressed the accelerator, and her truck zoomed past a pokey sedan. She throttled back on her temper and snuck a peek in her rearview mirror. No sense in adding a speeding ticket to her troubles.

"What do you mean, *again?*" asked Tess.

"I asked you first."

"He told me he's training your beast to fetch." A whistle

sounded in the background. "But so far I think they've got it backward."

Charlie clenched her fingers around the steering wheel. "Don't tell me he thinks he's staying for dinner."

"Okay, I won't. I'll let him be the bearer of the really bad news. I'm only the first-alert tattler here."

"And you play the part so well." Charlie exhaled a resigned-to-her-fate sigh. "I suppose I should thank you. Forewarned et cetera."

"You're welcome." Hardy barked again, and Tess laughed. "It was a tough choice between those annoying friendship duties and the pleasure of witnessing your reaction when you saw who was standing on your doorstep."

Charlie's face warmed at the thought of what Tess would have witnessed the night before. And it got warmer when she realized that Tess would probably figure out everything the moment she got a look at Charlie's pink cheeks and Jack's cocky grin.

"You need to pick up some beer on your way home," said Tess.

"There was plenty in my fridge last time I looked."

"That was before one of your dinner guests played hostess in your absence."

Charlie muttered a curse, disconnected and tossed the phone on the bench seat with a frustrated growl. A few kisses, and Jack thought he could just ooze into her life like slime. Like an amoeba on slime.

An amoeba with a talent for kissing.

She pulled into the tiny lot of Kessler's convenience store

a few blocks from her house and dashed inside to get the beer.

"Seems like just yesterday I was asking for your ID," said Stan Kessler as he took her cash.

Charlie crammed the receipt and change into her pocket. "Wasn't all that long ago."

"Long enough. Couldn't tell by your mom these days, though. The years don't seem to have hardly touched her any."

"Is that so?" Something about the speculating smile on Kessler's face trapped Charlie at the counter. She waited for his answer with the sinking feeling that she wasn't going to like whatever gossip was headed her way.

CHAPTER FOURTEEN

CHARLIE WAITED IMPATIENTLY while Stan settled his elbows on the counter in his rumor-spreading pose. "Sue Benson tells me your mom's been spending a lot of time with a good-looking man lately."

"Ben Chandler? He's just a friend."

"Seems to spend a lot of time at her house. Was there all of Sunday afternoon, and then again Monday night, I heard."

Her mother had spent last night with Ben? And then she'd shown up at the office looking for a job.

God. Her mother had come down with a raging midlife crisis.

"Nothing like a new boyfriend to put a certain bounce in a woman's step, I always say." Stan gave Charlie a knowing smile. "Keeps her young, too."

Charlie mumbled her thanks for the beer and made a quick getaway. She headed down the street toward her house and slammed on her brakes when Hardy dashed through the headlight beams and disappeared up her driveway, a red frisbee clamped in his teeth.

Swearing under her breath, she pulled in after him and climbed from her truck, bracing for his welcome-home dance-and-prance routine. But her dog was more interested in a wrestling match on the lawn with Jack.

With long-limbed, lean-muscled, devilishly dimpled, outrageously handsome Jack Maguire. Who had come to see *her,* plain and scrawny Charlie Keene. Again.

Of course, this visit might be strictly business.

She pulled the beer from the truck and stalked toward him. "You again?"

He rolled to his side and took hold of Hardy's collar to keep the dog from licking his face. "Is that any way to greet the only man capable of teaching this mutt some Southern manners?"

"That would explain the basic communication problem," called Tess from her observation post on the porch steps. "That dog only speaks Yankee."

Jack stood and brushed redwood needles from his grass-stained jeans. A twig hung from his messy hair, and Charlie itched to pluck it loose and then run her fingers through the thick, dark blond waves to mess him up some more.

Okay, maybe she'd allow herself one last kiss before she sent him on his way. If he behaved and didn't eat more than his share of pizza. "Hi," she said with a shy smile.

"That's better." He grinned back at her, stealing her breath. "Hi."

"Oh, *brother.*" Tess shook her head at the two of them. "You're sleeping together, right?"

"Wrong." Charlie shot Jack a warning glance and turned toward the house. "Let's eat."

He captured her arm as she started toward the door. "Thanks, but I'm not staying."

"But I thought you—"

"Not tonight. You've got plans, and I—" His gaze touched briefly on each of her features, as if he were taking some kind of personal inventory. "I shouldn't keep you from them."

He released her arm and hooked his thumbs in his pockets. "Night, Tess," he called. "Thanks for the hospitality."

"Anytime." She lingered on the porch, but after a long, meaningful glance from Charlie, she whistled for Hardy and followed the dog into the house.

So, this was it. The moment Charlie had dreaded. He hadn't come for dinner—he'd come to dump her. Not that they were dating. A dinner and a movie—on two separate evenings—didn't exactly qualify as a relationship.

She gazed at his beautiful face, taking an inventory of her own.

"You're welcome to stay," she said at last, hoping she sounded polite instead of pleading.

"I appreciate that." He plucked the twig from his hair, and his lopsided smile told her he was struggling with his decision. "But like I said, you've got things to do, and I'd be a mighty tempting distraction if I stayed."

"Not that tempting."

"But a distraction."

"For Tess, maybe."

His smile widened.

"All right." She sighed heavily, concealing her delight. "You're a distraction. A total disaster, a threat to any situation. A walking apocalypse where my concentration is concerned."

"Glad to hear it." He stroked a fingertip down the length of her nose and tapped the tip. "Same goes."

Her pulse stuttered. "How sweet."

"Thought you'd appreciate the sentiment." His smile faded. "I'd sure like to kiss you before I go, but I have the feeling we've got ourselves an audience."

"I'm sure you're right."

"Well, then," he said, swiping at his clothes. "I'll just excuse myself and let you see to your dinner guest. Night, Charlie."

"Night."

Tess was at the window, watching Jack pull from the curb when Charlie entered the house. She let the curtain fall back into place. "That man is seriously cute," she said. "And hot."

Charlie gave her a black look as she headed toward the back of the house, nudging Hardy out of her way. "Whose side are you on, anyway?"

"Maybe we don't have to choose sides," said Tess as she followed Charlie into the kitchen. "Like I said, maybe we can simply toy with him while he's here. Take turns breaking his heart and then kick him to the curb when it's time for him to pack his bags."

"Yeah. Right."

"I saw the thing he did with your nose," said Tess. "So, have you slept with him yet?"

Charlie dropped the beer on the kitchen counter. "I told you, he's here to put my fam—"

"I know, I know. He's here to end all life on the planet." Tess grabbed paper goods from a drawer. "But I bet he's dynamite in bed. Bet he kind of slides around the subject and takes his time getting to the point, extra slow and sweet, like the way he talks." Tess shivered. "Gives me goose bumps just thinking about it."

Charlie took a dog biscuit from her cookie jar and held it out of Hardy's reach. "I wouldn't know. And I don't care."

"But how does he kiss?" Tess pointed at Charlie's face. "A blush. I knew it. I knew there was something going on between the two of you."

"There's nothing going on." Charlie opened the back door, tossed the biscuit into the yard and shut Hardy outside so they could eat in peace.

"Kissing is not nothing," Tess said. "Kissing is something. A big something, if there's plenty of it." She reached into the refrigerator and helped herself to a diet cola. "So, spill. What's his style? Slow and sizzling? Hot and wild? Limited to the lips, or wandering out-of-bounds? A little snorkeling near the surface or some serious deep-sea diving?"

"I don't know." Charlie shrugged at Tess's impatient humph and pried a beer can from its plastic ring. "Kind of...all of the above, I guess."

"A man of many talents." Tess grinned. "I hope you appreciate what you've got."

"I haven't got anything. I don't want anything, especially not from Jack Maguire. What I want at the moment is pizza and party planning."

"Yes, sir. Sheesh," said Tess as she opened the take-out box on the kitchen table. "Bad day?"

"Let me give you the highlights." Charlie pulled a slice from the pizza and slapped it on a paper plate. "My brother seems to have disappeared, my mother is having an affair, and the man who is ruining my career is also alienating my dog's affections."

"Maudie's having an affair?"

"According to Stan Kessler."

"Wow." Tess lifted her soda in a salute. "Go, Maudie."

Charlie stared at her. "That's all you have to say?"

"She's not my mother." Tess sipped her drink. "I get to be jealous instead of mortified."

"Shit," said Charlie as she dropped into her chair. "I think I'm jealous, too."

"EXCUSE ME, AGATHA," said Jack as he pulled out his BlackBerry and checked the screen during Wednesday's breakfast. "I'll take this in the hall."

He walked around the corner and headed toward the relative privacy of the entry area. "Good morning, Miss Sally."

"If only it were true. Listen, Maguire, I think Bill's getting ready to pull out of this one."

"Bill?" Jack sighed and took a seat on Agatha's dainty entry settee. Things must be going from bad to worse down in the city. "He's never gone weak-kneed on one of my deals before."

"He's never been faced with the possibility of losing his job before, either."

Damn. Jack leaned an elbow on a knee and rubbed his forehead. "If it happens, it won't be my fault."

"Exactly." She paused for a loud sip of coffee as her fax machine whined in the background. "Your assignment is one of the few things he can control at the moment. And believe me, with the rumors zinging around here right now, the safe move is looking like the smart move."

"Whatever happened to the philosophy of big risks leading to bigger rewards?" Bill had shared that one with Jack over whiskeys at the local pub when they'd first started working together—how many years ago? Bill's youngest had been eleven. She was in high school now, Jack thought.

"Sentiments like that are *so* last week," said Sally. "Just ask your good buddy Noah."

"I've never pushed things so far they didn't snap back." And made some nice piles of money for everyone involved, he added silently.

"Well, we're all feeling a little snappy and snippy at the moment." Sally sucked in a big breath and let out a bigger sigh. "Look, Jack, Bill's got a designer wife and three expensive kids. He's not going to risk all that on a complicated buy with a questionable payoff."

Jack slumped against the settee's carved back. "You pulling out on me, too?"

"Never. You're the man. You're my hero, blah, blah, blah."

Jack grinned. "I miss you, Sally."

"Yeah? So prove it, and get your butt back here before it gets kicked out of some other butt's way."

"Maybe I will." He stood and started back toward the dining room. "I'll call Bill, talk this over with him."

Looked like he'd be spending the day holed up in the San Marcos suite, rushing through his report on the paperwork Sawyer had provided and trying to communicate his enthusiasm for the deal in the margins. Time was growing short, now that Maudie Keene seemed to be taking a more active interest in the family business. And the moment Charlie managed to get Maudie and David in line, Jack had no doubt she'd quickly be able to put her hands on the cash necessary to buy out her competition.

BayRock was a gem of a find, a true hot prospect. A relatively debt-free and viable business with a healthy customer base—an opportunity anyone would be tempted to snap up.

Anyone.

"Want me to put you through?" asked Sally.

"No." He peeked around the corner into the dining room and caught a scolding look from Agatha. "I'll try him later."

He slid his BlackBerry out of sight and mumbled an apology as he took his place at the table. He nodded and smiled and made the correct responses to the morning's conversation, but he'd lost his appetite. He was contemplating an adjustment in his career plans—and all the risks involved.

MAUDIE STEPPED FROM BEHIND a display of antique cameras when the bell above the entrance to the County Museum jingled. "Geneva," she said with a smile. "How are you?"

"Fine. As always." Her friend set her slender clutch purse near the reception log and began to unbutton her cashmere coat. "No visitors, I see."

"There rarely are on a Wednesday." Maudie set her feather duster near Geneva's purse. "And I have to admit, I've begun to like it this way."

"Alone with your thoughts?"

"I don't have to come here to be alone," said Maudie. "But that may change."

Geneva raised an eyebrow and then shrugged out of the coat and draped it over the back of the receptionist's chair. "If you're looking for another reason to get out of the house, I could use some help with the annual University Foundation wine tasting. Someone to manage one of the stations."

"Oh, my." Thrilled with the invitation to be part of one of Carnelian Cove's most elegant events, Maudie opened her mouth to accept. But in the next moment, her old insecurities smothered her response. What would she wear? What would she say if a stranger tried to strike up a conversation? "I-I'm not sure I'd be any good at that."

"Ben could help you."

"I don't know about that." The heat of a blush crept into Maudie's cheeks. Geneva approved of Maudie's relationship with Ben, her cousin by marriage, but she'd been careful not to interfere. "You could ask him," Maudie suggested.

Geneva raised her eyebrow again. "Why don't you ask him? I'm sure you see more of him than I do."

"I—" Maudie's face flamed red-hot, and she cleared her throat. "I don't see him that way—that often, I mean."

"Really? That's a shame." Geneva gave her a knowing look and then stepped past her, heading toward a recreation of a fussy Victorian parlor. She fingered the twisted gold fringe edging the velvet swagged across a false doorway. "Ben mentioned that he was seeing you."

"For business." Maudie clasped her hands together at her waist. "He's been giving me some advice. Good advice."

"I'm sure his advice is excellent." Geneva brushed the dust from her hands. "But he's got more to offer than financial advice, don't you think?"

"Yes. Of course." Maudie snatched the duster from the counter and crossed the entry to fuss over an arrangement of old shaving supplies. She wasn't ready to share the latest developments in her relationship with Ben with anyone. Not yet. Not until she'd figured things out for herself, at any rate. "He's a very generous man. Very kind."

"You're not a charity case, Maudie."

Maudie opened her mouth to respond but bit back the news about her new job. She was suddenly reluctant to share that, too. An uncomfortable silence filled the space between the two women, and Maudie began to wish this Wednesday were more like the others.

Geneva plucked a delicate china teacup from its saucer and examined the manufacturer's mark. "Jack Maguire came to see me two days ago."

"At Chandler House?"

"Yes." Geneva carefully set the cup back in place. "He's a very impressive young man."

"Charlie says he's here to put us out of business."

"I didn't know Charlie could be so melodramatic."

Maudie ran the duster over the player piano and

knocked a sheet of music to the floor. "He's been talking to Earl Sawyer."

"I hear he's been talking to Charlie and David, too."

"I don't know what to think." Maudie collected the music and stuck it back in place. "Those two have been going at each other worse than ever lately, snapping and growling like a couple of dogs fighting over a bone. And I'm the bone."

"Well," said Geneva, "I can see where Charlie gets her flair for drama."

Maudie snorted and gave the piano a final pass with the duster.

"Good thing you have Ben," said Geneva.

"No, I don't. Not really, anyway." Not after Monday night.

"Do you want to?"

"*Geneva.*" Maudie sank onto a settee. "You're embarrassing me."

"Why should you be embarrassed?" asked Geneva with a shrug. "If I were in your place, with an attractive man paying me all that attention, I'd be delighted. And, quite frankly, somewhat grateful."

Maudie stared at her hands clasped in her lap. "I'm not…ungrateful, exactly."

"Then what are you, exactly?"

"Not ready."

"When will you be ready?"

"I don't know."

"Well, if you don't know," said Geneva, "then no one does."

Maddie glanced at her friend. "I don't want to hurt him."

"Then don't." Geneva wandered toward the entrance to stare at the street. "What do Charlie and David think of Ben?"

"Charlie approves of him, but only because she thinks he agrees with her business decisions. I don't think David pays enough attention to have an opinion."

"Or maybe he's ignoring the situation."

"There's no situation to ignore." Maudie stood and retrieved her feather duster. "I know Ben is a wonderful man. And I know how lucky I am that he cares for me. Really, I do. But until—until recently, there was only one man in my life. And I was married to him for thirty-three years."

"You had a wonderful life with Mitch. I imagine that makes it hard to think you could recapture what you had with someone else."

"No, it wouldn't be the same. I'm not the same person I was." Maudie fingered the duster. "The thing is, I don't think I'm ready to settle into that old pattern again. Not for a while, anyway."

Geneva smiled. "I guess I'm the last person who has the right to comment on that topic."

Maudie laughed and brushed her duster over a Victrola.

"There's another reason I stopped by today," said Geneva. "I wanted to warn you to be careful with Jack Maguire. Very, very careful."

"What do you mean?" Maudie pressed a hand to her stomach. "Is Charlie right? Is he going to cause trouble?"

"He's certainly capable of it." Geneva opened the visitors' log to the last page of entries. "He strikes me as a clever and determined young man. A man who can figure out a way to get whatever it is he wants."

"So we have to make him want to go away."

"Yes, it may be that simple." Geneva turned another page and glanced at Maudie. "Is that what you want? To make him go away?"

"I don't know." Maudie squeezed the duster's handle. "I haven't met him."

"As I said, he's very impressive. Very…persuasive." Geneva closed the book. "But then, I think you can deal with a persuasive man. You seem to be doing just fine dealing with Ben."

"I told you," said Maudie, meeting Geneva's assessing gaze. "I'm not dealing with him."

"Maybe that's the problem."

Maudie kept her mouth shut.

"Another reason I came by this morning," said Geneva, "was to see if you'd like to come to Chandler House for dinner on Saturday night."

"Thank you—I'd love to."

"I'm having a little party, so wear something fun." She paused. "Ben will be there."

Maudie lifted an eyebrow. "Matchmaking, Geneva?"

"I'll wait to see whether it's successful before I take credit."

"A wise policy."

"It's served me well for many years." Geneva pulled her coat from the chair and slipped her arms into the sleeves. "So, you won't mind if he's there?"

"Not at all. No problem." Maudie waved the feather duster beneath her chin. "*That* I can deal with."

CHAPTER FIFTEEN

CHARLIE STALKED INTO THE reception area shortly after eleven on Wednesday morning. "Gus, have you—"

"No, I haven't heard from David." The dispatcher leaned back in his chair. "But I have an idea where you might find him."

"Me, too." She sucked in a deep breath and let it out slowly, ordering herself to be calm and rational and patient. To be an understanding sister. David couldn't be happy about their mother's decision to keep Keene Concrete in the family, and he'd deserved some time to lick his wounds in private.

That time was up. "Guess I'll head out for a long lunch today," she said. "See you when I get back."

"What do you want me to do with Maudie if she shows up before you do?"

"Shit." Charlie set her hands on her hips and blew out a frustrated sigh. "I don't know. I don't know what I'm going to do with her, either. Call me when she gets here, and tell her I'm on my way."

Too bad she couldn't send her mother after David, thought Charlie as she drove through the gate and headed toward the highway. It would have saved a lot of time today.

Time. She was running out of it. If she couldn't convince her mother and David to go along with her on the BayRock purchase and sign the paperwork to start the loan process, Earl would lose patience and sell to Continental.

Twenty minutes later she rolled to a stop behind David's car, which was parked beside an aging warehouse at the abandoned rail spur. A friend had loaned him the use of the building for his sculpting. The lighting was poor, but he had space and ventilation.

She stepped out through the open doorway and waited for her eyes to adjust to the dim interior. "David?" she shouted over the rock blaring from a portable speaker.

He stepped from behind a makeshift wall, wiping his hands with a grease-stained cloth, and flipped off the music. "What are you doing here?"

"I came to ask you the same question." She scuffed her boot over a crack in the concrete floor. "And to ask how you're doing."

"I haven't slit my wrists, if that's what you were wondering."

"So…you're doing okay."

"Yeah." He scrubbed at a speck on one of his hands. "I'll survive."

"Glad to hear it." She walked toward a tall, airy arrangement of thick wires entwined with flashing triangles. "Nice."

"Thanks. It's the water feature for the new hotel."

"They want it?"

"I wouldn't be working on it if they didn't."

"Congratulations." She stared at the sculpture because

it was easier than looking at his shuttered features. "When were you going to mention it?"

"When it was closer to being finished."

"Sorry I ruined the surprise."

"What do you want, Charlie?"

"It's Wednesday." Charlie shoved her hands into her pockets. "The middle of the workweek. No one's heard from you since Monday."

"There weren't all that many orders on the schedule. I didn't figure you'd miss me."

"Well, you figured wrong." She walked to the other side of the sculpture to study it from a different angle, imagining how it might look with water splashing through the openings and cascading over the sharp metal edges. "Mom missed you, too."

"Mom?"

"She showed up yesterday, looking for a job."

"Mom?"

"Yes. Mom." Charlie shot him a bland look. "Maybe I should give her yours."

"Maybe you should."

He tossed the cloth on the table beside the speaker. "I want to go to school. To a real art school, the kind of school where I can learn what I need to know. And I can only do that in the city."

She sighed. They'd been through this so many times before. "David—"

"I've got talent, Charlie. And what's more, I've got the ambition to do something with it. You, of all people, should understand that."

The praise buried in his comment was such a surprise she didn't know how to respond.

"You've got a talent for business," he continued. "A natural ability to see how things will play out before they do. How to work out a compromise that makes everyone feel like they don't have to give up any more than the other guy." He leveled an accusing look at her. "Talent enough to keep me here much longer than I intended to stay."

She had to clear her throat twice before she could speak. "I didn't mean to make you unhappy."

"I know that. But I think it's time for us both to stop negotiating mutual sacrifices and look for a real solution."

"You've been talking to Jack, haven't you?" It was so much easier—so much more satisfying—to focus her frustration on the man who was turning her world upside down. "He talked you into this, didn't he?"

"No, he didn't. I haven't spoken to him since that first day. He knows who's really in charge at Keene, and it isn't me."

David stroked a hand down one of the triangles. "But you know what he did, Charlie? He listened. He didn't lecture me about how wrong I am to want this, or how crazy it is to think I can make it happen. He asked me questions about *how* I intended to make it happen, and then he listened to my answers. *He listened to me.*"

David paced across the room and turned back to face her again. "Do you know how much it means to have someone listen for a change?"

"Yes." She curled her fingers into fists inside her pockets and dug her nails into her palms.

"I don't want to hurt you, Charlie. I don't want to hurt Mom. I'm not doing this *to you*. I'm doing it *for me*." He muttered an oath. "I know that sounds selfish."

"In some ways." She sighed and sank into one of the folding chairs he'd set near the table. "It also sounds like it's the right thing to do—for you. Mom and I—we're not your family. I mean, not the family you're going to have someday. You need to go and find those people. You need to go and find the work that's going to make you happy. You were right," she said with a sad smile. "Of all people, I should understand how important it is to do work that makes you happy."

"I know Keene Concrete makes you happy. And you've got enough ambition to make it work without me."

She lifted her hands. "I can't afford to buy you out."

"Then talk Mom into selling to Continental. On the condition they keep you on as manager here."

"They'd never agree to that. And I don't want to work for anyone but myself."

"Neither do I," he said. "And yet I do it every day."

"You're an owner."

"But not the boss. No matter what title you let me put on my office door."

"If you would just sign the paperwork for—"

"No." He shook his head. "If I make it possible for you to go after BayRock, I'll never make it out of here. You'll have every asset tied up so tight I won't be able to pry a penny loose. And how will you double the company's size without my help?"

She stared at his stubborn expression, and then she slumped against the chair. "I'll figure something out."

"I'm sure you will." He gave her the first smile she'd seen since she walked in. "I'm counting on it."

"I'll miss you, David."

"I'll miss you, too."

"I'll really miss you every time Mom wants me to fix something at the house."

"You're better at that stuff than I am." He took the chair beside hers. "I always wonder why she calls me first."

"To make you feel needed, I suppose."

They sat in companionable silence, at peace with each other for the first time in months. Charlie soaked up the quiet and the feeling of contentment, storing it away for the long stretches of emptiness ahead.

CHARLIE PULLED INTO HER DRIVE after dark that night, switched off her truck's ignition and slumped in the seat. A storm had blown in late in the afternoon, and it hadn't let up yet. Fat raindrops spattered and streaked the windshield, blurring the faint light from her porch. She'd be soaked and chilled—again—before she made it through her front door.

Hardy needed his dinner. She needed hers, too, but she'd have to do more than pour kibble in a bowl. Maybe not. Maybe she'd do just that—dump a pile of cold cereal in a bow, douse it with milk and—

Milk. She'd forgotten to stop at Kessler's on the way home. She released a long, exhausted sigh and leaned her head against the seat, adding layers of disgust and self-pity to her mood.

A moaning gust of wind battered the truck and drove

the rain like gunfire against the metal. *Get moving. You can't sit here all night. The sooner you get going the sooner you can collapse in bed.*

And get an earlier start on all the fun tomorrow.

She shoved open the door and hunkered down to jog across her yard and climb her porch steps. Hardy's frantic dinnertime yelps grated at her as she fumbled with her key in the lock. "Coming. *Coming.*"

She tossed her wet jacket over the back of a chair in the front room, promising herself she'd collect it before it had time to dampen the upholstery, and trudged through the dining room into the kitchen. Numb with cold, she moved through her routine: unlock the back door, dodge Hardy, fill his bowl on the back doorstep, check his water.

"Always a thrill, isn't it?" she asked, watching him gulp his dinner as if she'd starved him for days. Poor Hardy. All that pent-up energy and no one to appreciate it. She'd make it up to him this weekend with a long run on the beach.

After the party. She groaned and turned to stare at the dirty dishes stacked on her counter and the dog hair clumped in the corners. She'd have to shovel out from under before Saturday night and work up some enthusiasm for entertaining her guests. Right now, just the thought of the coming chores seemed to drain the last of her strength.

Someone pounded on her front door, but Hardy was too busy choking down his last bite to raise the alarm. "Some watchdog you are," she muttered as she shut the door and made her way back through the house. She scowled at the pile of unread newspapers on the dining room table and decided her unexpected visitor would simply have to deal with her lousy housekeeping.

Her mood worsened when she yanked her door open to find Jack on her porch. "For cryin' out loud, when are you—"

"Save your breath," he said. "I know the drill. I'm the last person in the world you want to see, I'm making a pest of myself, I have no life. Well, neither do you, from what I've seen."

"If you think I'm inviting you in after that moving speech, you're dead wrong."

"Wouldn't be the first time." He edged past her. "Close the door before you let the bugs in."

"Too late." She took nasty pleasure in slamming the door and turned to glare at him. "And too bad I don't have any roach spray to deal with the one that just crawled in."

He ignored her remark and set a large brown take-out bag and a six-pack of beer on her locker-trunk table. "Dinner delivery."

"I didn't order any dinner."

"Not very hospitable of you," he said with one of his crooked grins, "considering that you were expecting company."

"And I'm not expecting any company."

"Not very observant of you, considering that the company has arrived." He glanced around the room. "Where's the assault dog?"

"Molesting the squirrels in the backyard."

"I suspected that dog had criminal tendencies." Jack

pulled a huge rawhide bone from the bag. "Good thing I showed up with a distraction."

He'd brought her dog a bone. Ridiculously touched, she stared at the bag, wondering what else was inside. Something as silly as carmel squares or as disgusting as that fish. "I don't suppose there's any way to make you leave."

"Probably. But I can't think what that might be at the moment."

"Figured there'd be a catch."

He carried Hardy's chew bone to the back of the house, and she peeked into the bag. Foil-wrapped grilled steak sandwiches and foam buckets of coleslaw from Alberto's. The peppery aroma of Al's seasoned fries and warm barbecue sauce tickled through her system, and her stomach burned in anticipation.

Jack's cursing punctuated the sounds of a brief scuffle, and then she heard the muffled *whump* of her back door closing. When he returned, he popped the top off a Paisley and handed it to her. "Hell of a day," he said.

"Hell of a week."

"Hell of a mess."

"You're the one who made it," she said after the first sip of cold ale had fizzed its way down her throat.

"Things around here were a mess before I pulled into town."

"And they'll probably still be a mess after you leave," she muttered.

He lowered the bottle he'd raised to his lips and tilted his head to the side with a frown. "What is it, Charlie?"

She blinked at the burn of threatening tears and wiped

the back of her hand across her mouth. "None of your concern."

"Here, now." He pressed a sandwich into her hands and gave her a gentle shove toward the pillows piled at one end of her sofa. "You look dead on your feet."

"What a nice thing to say. Thank you ever so much."

She didn't say another word as he took a seat beside her. He juggled his food with one hand while fiddling with the remote in the other, conducting a rambling commentary on their viewing choices. She leaned back, put up her feet and enjoyed her dinner, content to listen to his soft, low Southern babble and steal an occasional glance at his expressive features. Content with his easy-going company, even though it had been unexpected.

Soon she was satisfied, relaxed, warmed clear through and…happy. Why couldn't she find and hold on tight to this kind of simple happiness with a man? With *this* man? she thought as she snuck a peek at Jack's perfect profile.

Oh, well, no sense in yearning for the impossible. That kind of longing would drive her crazy.

"Thanks for dinner," she said as she crumpled her sandwich wrapper and tossed it on the trunk. "Drop by again sometime. Sometime next year, maybe."

"I sometimes wonder why I find that smart mouth of yours so irresistible." He tossed aside the remote and began to stuff the leftovers into the brown bag. "Especially since I'm not all that fond of some of the garbage that comes out of it."

"No one asked you to show up here tonight."

The grin he aimed at her over his shoulder was slow and

irritating and sexy as hell. "I'm not going anywhere," he said.

"That's what you keep saying."

"'Cause I'm still here."

She dropped her feet to the floor. "You can't stay forever."

"You seem to be counting on that."

"That's right."

"Well, it's starting to piss me off." He took her by the arm and turned her to face him. "What if I did stay?"

"You won't. You can't."

"What if I could?"

There was something in his unsmiling expression she'd never seen before, something potent and unnerving. She tugged herself free. "There's no point in thinking that way."

"Answer my question, Charlie."

"I'm too tired to play twenty questions with you tonight." And too tired to match wits with him—with the charm that shredded her resolve and the stubborn cheerfulness that deflected all her arguments. Too tired to resist this dangerous new intensity that had already heated her blood and sent it pounding through her worn-out body.

Slowly, steadily, his dark blue eyes locked on hers, he drew her close, closer, into his arms. She put up a halfhearted struggle, already softening against him. Wishing she'd slammed the door in his face when she'd seen him standing on her doorstep, looking cocky and handsome and too tempting by half. "I don't want to do this tonight," she said.

"Do what?" He lowered his face toward hers, and the warm, yeasty scent of ale washed over her features.

Her eyes fluttered closed. "This."

"This?" He brushed his lips over the tip of her nose, featherlight and oh-so-sweet. "Or this?" He trailed a path of silky kisses across her cheek and nipped at her earlobe.

"I—" She shivered when he blew in her ear, giving in, inch by inch. Wishing for the impossible, for her own piece of happiness, just for now. Just for tonight.

"How about this?" He slipped a hand beneath her sweatshirt as he nuzzled the spot behind her ear, and her spine turned to mush. "This might be nice."

"I don't want nice."

His fingers skimmed up her front and paused beneath her breast. "I could do naughty."

Oh, please, yes. "I'm sure you could."

"Just say the word."

"I—" It would be so easy, so simple to say yes. So wonderful to feel the way she knew he could make her feel. And so foolish to surrender to the moment, to her confusion and her exhaustion and her craving for contact. To surrender to her weakness, prolonging the inevitable.

He'd leave. She'd be hurt. Again. "I'm tired," she said.

"Yeah, well, I'm tired, too." He lowered his hand to her waist. "Tired of asking myself why I point my car in your direction each evening. Of asking why my first thoughts each morning are of you and how you might be scheming against me. Wondering what you might be up to. Wondering when I can see you and lay my hands on that delectable body of yours and kiss you breathless."

He pressed his lips to her forehead. "I sure do like kissing you, Charlie."

She closed her eyes, concentrating on his syrupy words and the warm weight of his hand at her side, ignoring the tiresome, nagging fact that he probably wouldn't be here next week. Counting on it, knowing everyone else expected it, too. This time, when a man left her, it wouldn't be her fault.

Just business. Nothing personal.

"I like kissing you, too," she said.

"Seems that's the one area where we're in complete agreement. Although it doesn't make things any easier." He rested his cheek against the top of her head. "I came here tonight to prove to myself that this whole wanting-to-kiss-you thing is crazy."

Crazy. The yearning, the wishing—foolish, all of it. *So very foolish.* Nearly as foolish as what she was about to do.

She grabbed the hem of his sweatshirt and began to wrestle it over his head. "So, did you prove it?"

"Yeah." He tugged his arms from his sleeves, and his hands streaked beneath her T-shirt to unfasten her bra. "It's crazy, all right."

"Glad you got that straight."

"Mmm." His warm, wide hands closed over her breasts, and the rough scrape of his calluses over her tender skin thrilled her. "How about you?" he asked.

"No problems here." No, no problems, not tonight. She grabbed handfuls of his thick, blond waves and leaned against him, sinking into another long, hot kiss and reveling in the slow burn of arousal pulsing through her system. "I always had it straight."

"Crazy, huh?"

"Totally." She ran the tip of a finger around one of his nipples and smiled when he groaned.

He shifted their positions and stretched over her. "You're not going to go and get all logical on me now, are you?" he asked as he lowered the zipper on her jeans.

"No." She arched against him when he cupped her, lost her place in the flow of the conversation when he stroked her with a leisurely rhythm, nearly lost her mind when he slipped a finger inside her and sent her close to the edge. "No, not here. Not like this."

They stood and stumbled toward her bedroom, struggling with laces and snaps and buttons and elastic, cursing and laughing between urgent, fevered kisses. She ran her hands over his body—the hard, muscled form of a man who'd labored for a living—desperate for more of the heat they could generate between them. He skimmed his fingers over her skin, caressing her curves, stealing her breath with the sweet affection of his touch. The touch of a man who took his time, who rambled through some interesting detours but always arrived where he'd meant to be.

The bed creaked and groaned as they fell onto it, the sheets rumpled and cool beneath their tangled limbs. Outside, Hardy's low howl answered a siren's wail, and a gust of wind rattled rose thorns against her window.

"I'm crazy about your hair," he said as he thrust his hands into it and held her steady for the slow, wet glide of his mouth over hers. She nibbled at his lower lip, and he smiled and nuzzled the side of her neck.

"I'm crazy about your smile," she whispered as she

traced the deep groove in his cheek. He turned his head and captured her finger in his mouth, sucking with a long, sensual pull before giving it a playful nip.

They rolled across the bed, and she shoved him against her pillow and pinned him beneath her. His broad chest rose and fell in a ragged syncopation, lifting and lowering her with each rough breath. He was slick with sweat, big and beautiful and solid and hers, all hers tonight.

"Your legs," he said as he ran a hand in a tickling, tormenting path from instep to thigh. "They drive me wild."

"Your voice," she murmured as she closed her teeth over one of his dark nipples. "It makes me insane."

He turned to his side and sprawled over her, making her writhe as he stroked from her neck to her center, drenching her in pleasure. On and on went his deep, lush kisses and those teasing, gliding touches, drawing out the anticipation until she sobbed with desire.

And then he slipped inside her, as easy and smooth as one of his dance steps, and she was content to follow his lead, to let him take her where he wanted her to go.

"I want you," he said.

"You've got me," she answered. Neither of them spoke again as the rhythm took them higher and pressed them closer and sent them flying.

CHAPTER SIXTEEN

JACK LAY BESIDE CHARLIE later that night, contemplating diamonds in rough patches. He'd arrived at her house tonight feeling as though the framework of his world was fracturing, and then, somehow, as he'd looked at her and argued with her and made love to her, all the jagged edges had fused into something new and vibrant and exciting. *This* was where he'd been heading, from the first moment he'd seen her in Sawyer's gravel yard. *This* was the deal he'd been after—this woman. The deal of a lifetime, if only he could figure out the angles and tally up the costs and decide on a successful opening bid.

Once the negotiations—and the courtship—began, he had no doubt of the outcome. He hadn't failed yet to close a deal.

He stared at the stucco patterns on her ceiling and analyzed the options for his next move. He figured he had to make a choice between what he wanted to do, and what he should do, and what he was expected to do, and what he needed to do. And he figured he'd better make that choice fast, before he fell asleep—which was what he was afraid he'd do.

"Jack."

"Hmm?"

"It's okay."

He turned to his side, facing her. "What's okay?"

"Leaving." She made a big show of a fake yawn and closed her eyes. "You can, you know."

"Why is it you're always reminding me I'm not going to be staying?" He tried to minimize the quick, neat stab of disappointment that she hadn't given him a nudge toward option number one—the thing he wanted to do, which was to pull her into his arms for another round of lovemaking. "Is that what you want me to do? To leave?"

Her shoulder moved in a jerky shrug. "If you want to."

He studied her pretty profile with a frown. She seemed so unaware of her appeal, so certain he'd take her up on her offer and duck out her door. Was that what the other men in her life had done? Had they made her doubt herself before dumping her like a leftover yard of slurry? If so, he'd like nothing better than to hunt each and every one of them down and give them a sample of old-fashioned, Southern-style corporal punishment.

If his theory was correct, he had one more very important reason to stay: to prove to her that he still wanted her.

And he did want her, enough to consider making some serious changes in his life. Enough to ditch the obstacles here, let Noah score his points and then take the vacation time he'd stored up and stick around Carnelian Cove for a while to see what might develop between them.

"The thing is," he said, "I don't know what to do about Agatha."

"Agatha?"

"I don't relish the idea of creeping through her front

door at the crack of dawn, wearing the clothes I wore the day before, and finding her in the kitchen working on my breakfast. Or knowing she'll climb the stairs tomorrow morning to make my bed and discover I didn't spend the night mussing the sheets."

"Why, Jack Maguire." Charlie shifted to her side, her nose a fraction of an inch from his. "You're a prude."

"Am not."

"Are so."

"I'm not a prude." He raised his head to punch his pillow into a more comfortable shape. "I've just got a certain…sensibility about matters like this."

"Mmm-hmm." Her lips turned up at the corners. "That explains why you haven't figured out yet why Agatha won't know what time you creep in. And why she'd never say a word about it, even if she did."

"And why is that?"

"I can't tell you." Charlie wiggled closer and brushed the tip of her nose over his. "I wouldn't want to do permanent damage to your sensibility."

He swung a leg over both of hers. "Tell me."

"Agatha won't notice what time you come in because she's probably busy mussing her own sheets with Kip Nielsen."

"Who?"

"Kip Nielsen. His fishing boat docked this afternoon, and after a pit stop at The Shantyman, he headed straight to Villa Veneto."

"What is it with this town?" asked Jack. "Do you all have spies at every corner?"

"No need to spy. Kip's a creature of habit, and that's his habit. Catch up on the news at the bar, shoot some pool with Phil and Russ and then make a quick hike to Oyster Lane."

"So Agatha's—"

"Nuh-uh-uh." Charlie pressed her fingers against his lips. "Give the lovebirds a little privacy."

"How long has this *habit* been going on?"

"Years and years."

"Why don't they get married?"

"I was right," said Charlie with a grin. "You are a prude."

"No, I'm not. But I like Agatha, and I don't like the idea of some man taking advantage of her."

"Believe me, no one takes advantage of Agatha." Charlie stroked a hand along his hip. "Kip's asked her to marry him, any number of times. But she keeps turning him down."

"I wonder why?"

"It's a mystery." Her fingers drifted along his side, over his shoulder and down his chest. "And it's sweet of you to care."

He caught her hand and brought it to his mouth. "That's 'cause I'm a man with a certain sensibility about matters like this."

"Certain sensibilities can come in handy at times."

He gathered her in his arms, having decided to return to the Villa Veneto much, much later. "Glad you noticed."

JACK'S BLACKBERRY RANG early the next morning as he strolled into his room, toweling his shower-damp hair. He tossed the towel on the bed and snatched the phone from Agatha's fussy nightstand. "Hey there, Sally."

"Your intuition is downright spooky." She paused for a noisy sip of coffee. "Moore just completed a successful bid for Continental."

Even though this news was expected, its impact should have sent a shock wave or two through his system. He raked his fingers through his hair, combing it out of his eyes, waiting for at least a ripple of apprehension.

Nothing.

He pulled a pair of jeans from the dresser. "Fair deal?"

"Rumor has it the board is *very* relieved."

Jack whistled as he struggled into his pants, one-handed. "It'll go fast."

"Like you-know-what through a goose."

Sally broke off for a moment to talk to someone in the office, and Jack slipped his watch over his wrist and checked the time. He needed to make some quick calls— Earl Sawyer, the airline, his accountant. He had to pack and talk to Agatha. Most of all, he needed to reach Charlie, to see her one more time before he left and explain where things stood. And where he wanted them to go.

After days of coasting at Carnelian Cove's vacation-like pace, Jack's stress level revved back up to city speed. He needed to process and compress too many important details into too few hours. Time—he'd kill for an extra dose of it today.

Time to get back to the basics.

"I'm back," said Sally. "That rustling sound you hear is résumés being pulled out and dusted off."

"Not mine."

She sighed. "I kind of figured that might be the case."

"Smart lady."

"I've got some intuition of my own."

"You've got spies."

"Best kind of intuition there is, around here." She paused for another sip of coffee. "I'm going to miss you, Jack."

"Same goes, Sally."

"So, what's going on up there?"

"Hard to tell." He glanced out the window and frowned at a misty soup growing thick and dark with the threat of rain. "It's fogged in, at the moment."

"I wasn't asking about the weather."

"I wasn't commenting on it."

"The sand-and-gravel lady giving you some trouble?"

"You could say that." He pulled a jacket from the narrow closet.

"Smart lady."

"You could say that, too."

"You know, Jack, there aren't too many guys who'd go out of their way to surround themselves with smart women."

"When it comes to women," he said as he tossed a pair of jeans on the bed, "I'd never settle for being just one of the guys."

He told Sally he'd check in after breakfast, and then he disconnected and stared out the window, wondering whether there'd be any flights out of the local airport in this weather.

Moore Enterprises may have made a friendly takeover bid, but all the corporate goodwill would stop dead at the payroll. There would be cuts—deep ones, he reckoned. Good thing he wasn't worried about his own job security.

No sense in worrying about a job he didn't want anymore.

He glanced at his phone and thumbed a familiar set of buttons. "Morning, Earl."

"Jack?" The rattle and roar of the plant nearly drowned Sawyer out. "You're up early."

"Hoping for a chance to talk to you this morning. Got time for a quick cup of coffee?"

Sawyer cleared his throat. "I don't know what there is to discuss."

"Well, now, I just might surprise you."

Jack mentioned a diner a mile or so down the road from BayRock, and Sawyer took the bait. They agreed on a meeting time, and Jack ended the call. "Might surprise myself, too," he said.

He'd definitely surprise Charlie, he thought as he punched in her number. And she wasn't going to like it one bit.

CHARLIE WINCED AS FREEZING spray from the rinse hose bounced off the mixer chute and soaked her thighs. Lenny kept his truck cab neat and the machinery shined—which Charlie appreciated—and she'd make sure he found mixer number thirty-six the way he'd left it when he returned to work next week. Lenny, a daddy. It was hard to wrap her mind around. She wondered how Trina's delivery was going. Gus hadn't radioed recently with an update from the hospital.

As she handed the hose over to one of the concrete finishers on the job site, the phone in her pocket buzzed. She fished it out with fingers numb from the cold and the wet. "Charlie here."

"Charlie, it's Ben."

He sounded serious—the news must be bad. Mom. David. She swallowed and tightened her grip on the phone. "Yes?"

"I just got off the phone with Geneva. Continental accepted a buyout offer this morning."

Oh God oh God oh God. "So, it's official. Hold on a minute, Ben." She dropped the phone in her pocket, folded the chute and latched it and then climbed into the cab where she could talk in private. "Does Mom know?"

"I called you first."

"Okay. Thanks, Ben. I'll let her know. And David." She thanked him again, disconnected and started the truck. It rumbled and vibrated around her, and warm, metallic-tasting air swirled through the cab. She hunched over the wheel, willing away the chills while she played out the coming scenes in her head. With David, who'd be resentful and sullen. With her mother, who'd be relieved his resentment was no longer aimed in her direction.

With Jack, who'd be leaving.

The pain sliced through her, unexpected and visceral. She sucked in a shaky breath and blinked hard against the sting behind her eyes. Ridiculous. Weak and stupid. He'd never said he wouldn't go. And how many times had she suggested he head back where he'd come from, sooner rather than later?

One week. It had been exactly one week since he'd shown up in Earl's gravel yard. One week since he'd first knotted up her stomach with that smile, seduced her with that charm and loved her like she'd never been loved before.

And she'd loved him back. Loved him. God, she *loved* him, and that hurt more than anything.

Well, she'd get over it. She'd get over him. Hell, there was nothing to get over, not really. A dance, a dinner date, a couple of shared snacks. A handful of kisses and one quick trip to the bedroom. Not exactly a relationship.

And now she could get on with business as usual, with her life as usual. She put the truck in gear and lumbered down the street, heading toward the plant. She'd call Earl when she got back—no, she should talk with David first.

Right now, she had a job to finish. She picked up the radio handset. "Thirty-six to base."

"Go ahead, Charlie," said Gus.

"Is David handy?"

"He's out on the loader. You want me to get him?"

The cell buzzed in her pocket. "No. It can wait. Tell him I want to meet with him when I get back to the plant. Thirty-six out."

She flipped her phone open. "Charlie here."

"Hey there, Charlie."

"Morning, Earl." She wondered what he knew—if he'd been in contact with Jack about the late-breaking news at Continental. If he was wondering, as she was, what this might mean for everyone—long-term and short-term—in Carnelian Cove. "Rain cleared up earlier than expected."

"Yep, and just in time for first-round deliveries." He paused and cleared his throat. "Hey, Charlie, I know I agreed to be patient until you could talk David and Maudie into signing on for the buyout financing but, well, something's come up."

She tightened her grip on the phone. "I hope it's something we can talk about, Earl."

"We can talk plenty, after Monday."

God, what now? She was too cold and hungry, too irritable with this scratchy, wet clothing and a nasty caffeine craving to deal with yet another crisis. And tired, so tired of dealing with so many things—and people—at once. "What's so special about Monday, if you don't mind my asking?"

"Maguire asked me to hold off till then."

"Is this something to do with Continental?"

"In a manner of speaking, I suppose." Earl hesitated again, and Charlie's stomach churned in the silence. "He said he'll have another offer for me to consider by then."

"Another—" Charlie braked for a stop sign. "What offer? What are you talking about?"

Had Geneva's source been mistaken? Had Continental pulled a fast one? Had Jack been fired—and was someone else about to be sent to do the dirty work in his place?

Or had Jack succeeded in seducing her out of the deal after all?

The car behind her blared its horn, and she crossed the intersection, spinning the wheel with one arm, angling out of the flow of traffic and heading to the curb. "Is this about the asking price? I thought we'd come to an agreement about how we were going to handle that."

"We did. I just… I feel like I owe him this chance, Charlie."

She stared, unseeing, out the windshield. "What chance is that?"

"The chance to put in his own bid for BayRock."

An icy, wicked burn began low in her gut and worked its way toward her throat. If he stayed, he'd be living in Carnelian Cove indefinitely. She'd be forced to deal with him every day. He'd become a permanent fixture in the only area of her life where she felt reasonably safe and secure: her work.

And when he dumped her and moved on—as a man like Jack would inevitably do with a woman like her—everyone would know all the details. Again.

Once again, she'd be subjected to those oh-so-sympathetic glances and murmurs. But this time—oh, this time she wouldn't be able to shrug away the hurt. This time the heartache would be real.

"Are you telling me what I think you're telling me?" she asked Earl.

"Jack's decided to quit Continental. He wants to move to Carnelian Cove and buy BayRock for himself."

CHAPTER SEVENTEEN

JACK HUNG HIS GARMENT bag on a hook in the back of his rental car and closed the door. He'd be driving his Porsche on the return trip. Not so roomy, maybe, but he'd enjoy cruising through the curves along the coast, and the trip would give him time to think.

He had a lot to think about.

He reminded himself to appreciate the adrenaline rush of a calculated risk. But the rush this time came with an unfamiliar twist in the gut and a strange pressure around the heart. It didn't ease his mind any that he'd be boarding his plane before he'd had a chance to talk to Charlie. But he needed to get to San Francisco with enough time left in the workday to put his plans in motion, and Gus had told him she was out for the morning on one of the mixers. Not the best circumstance for having a serious discussion about their futures.

Not that he knew exactly what he'd say to Charlie once he got in touch with her. How did a fellow tell a woman that he cared for her at the same time he was telling her he was scheming to become her number-one business competitor?

He shot one last glance at the Villa Veneto's fussy

exterior and grinned when he caught the twitch of a curtain in the bay window. Good old Agatha—nosy as ever. She'd told him she'd hold his room for him, and he hoped he wouldn't keep her waiting too long. With Sally's help, he'd wrap up most of the loose ends at Continental by the end of next week.

A white Keene mixer roared around a distant street corner at a terrifying speed, straightened with a jerk and headed in his direction as though it aimed to run him down. A cat slinking low-bellied across the road froze in stupefied panic, and the driver leaned on the froggy horn, the blare loud and long enough to rattle windows up and down Oyster Lane. Jack's instinct for self-preservation sent him hopping to the curb out of the truck's path as it shuddered to a stop inches from his car's front bumper, brakes whining and chassis groaning.

The cab door swung open and Charlie dropped to the pavement. She aimed that flamethrower stare of hers right at him, and he was sorely tempted to rub his hand over his heart again. But it was too late—he'd already been singed, but good.

He'd probably be catching some more heat in a moment. It looked like she'd already heard his news on the Carnelian Cove grapevine. *Damn*. He wished like hell he'd been able to tell her himself, but there hadn't been time to track her down on a job site. There wasn't time now to say what needed to be said.

"Mornin', Charlie." He slouched against his car. "Making a delivery in the neighborhood?"

"None of your business, Maguire." She swaggered

within slugging distance and then shoved her hands in her coverall pockets. Her hair hung in limp, wet spirals beneath her gimme cap, and her face was pale with cold beneath flecks of dark gray mud. "Going somewhere?" she asked.

"I s'pose I'd be justified in saying that's none of your business," he answered, "but that wouldn't be very polite now, would it?"

"Don't waste your time implying things about my manners in that sneaky way of yours." She batted at a stray curl tickling her cheek. "Answer my question. Going somewhere? Like, back to San Francisco, maybe?"

"Maybe." He hitched one shoulder in a casual shrug. "I s'pose the possibility makes you want to dance for joy, seeing as how you've been urging me to do just that since the moment we met."

The flash of pain in her eyes surprised and unsettled him, and he cursed himself for both reactions. He should have tried harder to reach her this morning, to be more careful with her and with whatever it was that had sprung up between them—this strange something that clogged his thoughts and choked off his words and made it hard for him to concentrate on what he needed to do and say.

"Why start being cooperative now?" she asked. "You know what they say—stick with what you know."

"Now, where's the fun in that?"

"This is just a game to you, isn't it?" She tossed up her hands. "It's all about winning, any way you can."

The fact that she could still think that about him after what they'd shared last night nearly brought him to his knees. "Talked to Earl, did you?"

"Yeah, I talked to Earl." She began to say something else, but she stumbled over a hitch in her breath.

"Charlie." Terrified that the moisture welling in her eyes might spill over and mortify them both, he straightened and reached for her. But then he froze, all too aware of Agatha behind the curtain and the scene they were making in the middle of the street.

This was no place and no time to start this discussion. He had a plane to catch, and she was late for the next delivery, and… *"Damn."*

Charlie backed away. "You weren't going to call before you left. You weren't going to tell me about your—your change in plans."

"No." Her disbelief and resignation cut him clean to the bone. She didn't believe him, didn't trust him. "That's not true. I tried."

"Not hard enough." She wiped the back of her hand across her mouth, but he'd already caught a glimpse of her trembling lip. "Well, it doesn't matter now," she said.

"Yes, it does." He chanced a step toward her. "It's not just about the business anymore."

"You're right about that, Maguire. Now it's personal."

"That's right," he said, trying to work up a grin and failing miserably. "We've got ourselves a relationship here."

"Relationships are built on more than sex. We don't have anything."

"We could." He ran his fingers through his hair, frustrated with this stilted attempt to communicate. "I want us to try."

"Figures." She nearly spat the word at him. "That's

what you do, Jack. You want. You collect things. You get them, you *acquire* them." She threw her arms wide. "Okay, you got me. You *had* me. Now what? What do you usually do with the things you get? Oh—I remember now. You take them apart and get rid of the pieces you don't want anymore. The things that don't matter at the moment."

"That isn't me. That's not what I do."

"Pardon me. It's the people you work for who take care of that part. You've already moved on to the next job, looking for the next thing to pick up and pass along."

"Maybe I want to stay put and figure things out for myself this time."

"Maybe." Her breath hitched again and she seemed to collapse in on herself. "Now there's a word loaded with a world of hurt."

"Or a world of possibilities."

"Yeah, you've been conditioned to see the possibilities in a deal—and then pass them along to someone else."

He glared at her. "I'm not going to apologize for being good at what I do."

"I didn't ask you to."

"What are you asking, Charlie?"

He waited, but she pressed her lips together.

"Must be nice to be so sure of everything," he said. "So sure of what everyone else should do. Most days, I'd settle for knowing what's right for me."

He shoved his hands into his pockets. "I'd thought I was about to make a pretty good deal here, but I guess I was wrong."

She shook her head as she backed toward the truck. "You won't win, you know. I won't let you."

"So you've told me, more than once. But I don't see how you can stop me, not this time."

She climbed into the cab and stared down at him. "Maybe I won't be able to stop you. But I can still keep you from winning, in the end."

He stood in the street, watching her drive away.

FIVE HOURS LATER, JACK fingered his tie as he strode down the hall toward Bill Simon's office. Wouldn't do to hand in his resignation with a crooked knot. He peered through the open doorway. "Bill?"

"Jack. Come in." The balding, ruddy-faced man gestured vaguely toward one of the black leather chairs arranged in a corner. "Glad you're back. Hell of a time to be away."

Jack settled in the chair closest to Bill's desk and decided not to remind his boss he'd given his blessing to Jack's trip and waved him on his way. "How're things in the LA office?" asked Jack.

"Panic time."

"Any cause for it?"

"No one knows. No one's going to know anything until something happens." Bill spread his hands. "And no one knows when that'll be."

"Business as usual in the meantime, I s'pose."

"For some of us, anyway." Bill picked up a rubber band and stretched it between his fingers as he swiveled back in his chair. "Rumor has it you're thinking of leaving us."

Jack stared at the envelope in his hand. In this quiet office with the pewter-toned carpet and the smoky window glass and the jet-black office furniture, the color and noise of Carnelian Cove seemed a world away. "Yep."

"You knew before you left that the northern California deal was a stretch."

"That's right."

"But then, you've always liked going after the riskier prospects."

"And proving they weren't so risky after all."

Bill nodded slowly in acknowledgment. "Which is why I hope that envelope doesn't contain what I think it does."

Jack returned his boss's steady gaze. "I guess my timing was a little off with this particular prospect. It couldn't have been the risk factor. Not with my record."

Bill ignored the barb. "I never thought you'd let Noah push you into doing something like this."

"No pushing involved. I'm jumping. Been considering it for some time now. Just happened to find a good place to land."

"What if I asked you to hold off for a while," said Bill, "until the dust settles around here?"

"Business as usual?"

Bill tossed down the rubber band with a sigh. "Noah made a damn good case for backing away from Carnelian Cove. Solid analysis, taking into account a number of current market variables. But when it came down to it, it had nothing to do with the buyout. The Carnelian Cove operation simply doesn't suit our needs at this time."

"I'm glad Noah made such a strong case, as it turns out." Jack slid the envelope onto Bill's desk. "Turned out best for all concerned."

Frowning, Bill picked up the envelope. He opened it, read the letter and dropped it on his desk. "I don't suppose I can get you to file this away for a month or so, see what pops with the reshuffle. You're well positioned to make a significant move here."

"I've got another move in mind." Jack leaned back and crossed an ankle over one knee. "And I've got some vacation coming. Sally can help Noah pick up the slack."

"Does Sally know you're making this suggestion?"

"Yep." Jack smiled for the first time in several tense, difficult hours. "She probably figures she'll have Noah's job inside a year, anyway."

Bill snorted out a humorless laugh and swiveled to stare out his window at the cityscape below. "What are you going to do?"

"Head back north."

"And run a small-time sand and gravel operation?"

"It suits my needs at this time."

Bill frowned. "Waste of your talent."

"I've got more than one talent," said Jack, his smile widening. "And plenty up there to keep me on my toes."

"Think Sally'll come after your outfit in a few years?"

"I'd be disappointed if she didn't give it a try."

Bill stood to extend his hand across his desk. "I've enjoyed working with you."

"Same goes," said Jack as rose to take it.

Bill picked up the rubber band again. "Why do I get the

feeling there's more behind this decision of yours than you're letting on?"

"Because there is." Jack shoved his hand into his pocket. "Charlie Keene, part owner of Keene Concrete."

"Mitch Keene's daughter?"

"Yep."

"Hear she's a tough customer."

"That's right."

Bill's face eased into a grin. "I'd like to see the risk-management analysis on that particular business move."

Jack tugged at his tie. "I'm working on it."

CHARLIE DUMPED THE LAST bag of chips into her largest mixing bowl on Saturday night and elbowed her way through the crowd to deposit it on the makeshift buffet in her front room. A Radiohead hit blasted from the speakers one of Tess's friends had dragged in from his van, competing with shouted conversations and amplified laughter. She'd never understood why a party's success could be gauged by the decibel level, but she was glad Addie's birthday bash was deafening—and even more glad it was nearly over.

Tess grabbed her arm and leaned in close to yell in her ear. "We're running out of limes."

Charlie shook her head. "I stashed some extras in a bag above the refrigerator."

"I'll find them," said Tess. "You deal with the guy who just walked in your front door."

Charlie turned to see Jack squeeze past two of Addie's guests and duck into the hall, headed for the back room.

He was carrying a small box wrapped in sunny yellow paper and a handful of pink roses tied with a gauzy pink bow—he looked tired and grim and so handsome she longed to wrap her arms around him and make them both feel better.

She caught up with him in the spare bedroom as he shrugged out of his jacket and tossed it beside the others on the bed. "What are you doing here?"

"I was invited."

"By Tess?"

"And Addie."

"So it's a conspiracy."

Charlie stepped aside as a former high school classmate and his wife came through the door to collect their things. She played the proper, patient hostess as they thanked her for the party, though the music pounded through her aching head and set her teeth on edge. She smiled and nodded and said good-night, while Jack stared at her with a dangerously impassive expression, and she wanted him with every cell in her body.

He stood, motionless, waiting until the couple had left and he and Charlie were alone—as alone as possible with a couple of dozen people crammed into rooms a few feet away.

"I like your friends," he said at last. "And apparently, they like me."

"Isn't that convenient. Must be because you're such a friendly guy."

"Maybe so. That explanation is a whole lot simpler than that conspiracy theory of yours."

The music changed tempo, from take-me-baby to I-dare-you-to-try. Why couldn't she think of something clever or dismissive or meaningful to say? And why did he have to choose this moment to go silent and broody?

He lifted the box and flowers from the dresser. "I brought Addie a present."

"You didn't have to do that."

"I know. I didn't have to bring these flowers as a hostess gift, either, but it appears I've developed an annoying habit of attending to the niceties in social situations."

"It's not annoying." It was wonderful. *He* was wonderful, damn him. And the flowers were gorgeous.

He raised an eyebrow and continued to stare at her with that infuriatingly shuttered look—the one she recognized as one of his many versions of stubborn. He slowly extended the flowers.

"Okay, you're right. It's annoying." She snatched the flowers from his hand and resisted the urge to bury her nose in their sweet, heady perfume. No one had brought her a bouquet since her disastrous high school formal. "Annoying and—" Her throat closed up for a terrifying moment. "And wonderful. And that's what makes it so annoying."

She sat on the edge of the bed and plucked at the edges of the ribbon. "Did you come all this way just for Addie's party?"

"And to leave my car here. I'll be staying with Agatha while I look for a house."

She swallowed a nasty surge of panic. "A house?"

"I'm staying, Charlie. I've quit Continental." He moved

toward the door and then turned to face her. "I'm going to get my own place, not a piece of someone else's. My own place, my own piece of Carnelian Cove. Guess you'd better start getting used to the idea."

CHAPTER EIGHTEEN

MAUDIE STEPPED OUT ON Geneva's terrace Saturday night and gasped at the cold, drawing her new pashmina shawl more tightly around her arms. Choosing a sleeveless, low-backed dress for the dinner party had seemed a daring idea, but it was also impractical for this time of year. "Hello, Ben."

He turned at the sound of her voice, and the look on his face was worth every goose bump. "Maudie?"

"Yes. It's me." She walked toward him and tipped up on her toes to give him the kind of air kiss she'd seen in the movies. The familiar scent of his cologne tempted her to linger right where she was, but she shifted back and lifted her champagne flute for a sip. "How are you, Ben?"

"Fine." His gaze traveled her length, taking in her sky-high heels and her at-the-knee hemline, sexy new hairstyle and the glittering necklace at her throat. "Just fine."

She moved to the balustrade and stared into the backlit garden. "It's so lovely here, in any season."

"Yes. It is."

She waited for him to touch her, to put his hands on her shoulders, to turn her around, into his arms, to lower his mouth to hers. To tell her how much he'd missed her, how much he wanted her back. She grew warm imagining the scene and willing it to happen. But all she felt was another cold breeze, and she wondered how much longer she'd last out here before she began to shiver.

She tossed back her hair with a tiny shake of her head. "I wonder if Geneva appreciates her views the same way her visitors do, considering that she sees them every day."

"I'm sure she must, since she supervises every square inch of this place."

Maudie laughed and gave her hair another playful toss. "She's always had more energy than any three people I know."

"Maudie."

"Yes?"

"Did you come out here to talk about Geneva?"

She donned a brilliant smile and turned. "I came out here to see the view from the terrace."

"I'm glad you did." He stepped toward her. "You've improved the view one hundred percent."

"Thank you."

"You look different tonight."

"I feel different."

He swallowed and stared at his empty flute. "I heard you've started working at Keene Concrete."

"News travels fast, doesn't it?"

"Do you like it?"

"Not yet. But I'm not going to quit until I find something better."

He glanced up with a smile. "And when you do find it, then you'll quit?"

She laughed a little too gaily. "That didn't come out quite right, did it?"

He stepped closer. "Am I making you nervous?"

"No," she said, although something about the way he'd moved closer and his soft, low voice had stolen her breath for a moment. "I'm cold."

"Then you should go back in."

"Are you coming in, too?"

"In a minute."

"Oh." She frowned and tugged awkwardly at her wrap with one hand while trying not to spill her champagne. She wished now that she hadn't taken it from the server. She didn't really care for champagne, and she'd rather have had something else—anything else—to drink.

"Here," said Ben, reaching for her glass. "Let me help you with that."

"Thank you." Her frown deepened as he stood, silent and much too far from her, holding the glasses like a patient, indifferent butler while she fussed with her wrap.

He'd said he found her attractive. Wasn't he dying to touch her?

He'd said she looked different. Was she too different to appeal to him?

She'd run out of conversation and excuses. All she wanted now was to escape. "Thank you," she repeated, reaching for her glass.

He lifted it out of range. "I'll take care of this for you."

"Pardon me?"

"You don't like champagne, Maudie."

It took her a moment, but then she realized she'd made

that comment once at a wedding they'd attended. He'd remembered. *Oh, Ben.*

"Thank you," she said yet again, because she couldn't think of anything else to say. Her hair fell over her forehead, annoying her. And her left foot was cramping inside the tight shoe.

He cocked his head to the side. "You seem very grateful tonight."

"And different," she said with a slight pout.

"Yes, that, too."

"Well, th—" She frowned. "I'm going now."

"I'll see you inside."

She turned to go and glanced over her shoulder. "Aren't you cold, too?"

"Freezing."

"Why don't you come in and sit by the fire with me."

"I need to stay out here a while longer."

"Why?"

"Maudie." He carefully set the glasses on the top rail. "Are you going to force me to explain the difficulties of the male anatomy to you?"

"Do you mean you're—"

"Yes, Maudie." He slipped his hands into his pockets. "I'm very, *very* glad to see you."

Embarrassed, she covered her mouth to hide her smile. "I'm sorry."

"Don't be. This is the most excitement I've had all week."

"That's your fault," she said.

"Is it?"

"I want a lover, Ben."

"I want a wife."

She sighed and shoved an errant wave out of her eyes. "I've made so many changes in my life over the past few days. I want to have some time to enjoy all the new feelings that have come with them."

"And you can't do that while planning for a wedding?" He took a step closer. "Shopping for a ring? Looking at different honeymoon locations?"

She smiled. "Are you trying to bribe me?"

"Is it working?"

"I have to admit, you've captured my interest."

"That's a start." He closed the gap between them and framed her face in his hands. "You know, a long engagement might be a good idea. It would give us plenty of time to find a new house."

"A house?" She laughed and wrapped her fingers around his wrists. "You're not playing fair."

"I'll do whatever it takes to get you to agree to marry me."

She bit her lower lip. "Would you make love to your fiancée while she considers your other offers?"

He heaved a put-upon sigh. "If I must." And then he lowered his lips to hers and pulled her against him, holding her tight, warming her all the way through.

JACK ENJOYED A GOOD party. The pumped-up noise that thrummed beneath the skin, the flow of bodies and the undercurrents of conversations, the faces lit with excitement and laughter, the loosened inhibitions and the possibilities that came with them.

This party had been filled with possibilities—and pockmarked with land mines. He slouched against a wall, sipping his beer and pretending to listen to Dale Trumble, one of Charlie's neighbors, give Addie the inside scoop on the recent layoffs at the mill. And pretending not to notice how hard Charlie was trying to ignore him, and how hard Tess was trying to ignore her ignoring him, and how hard Addie was trying to entertain him so he could ignore the whole situation.

"Well," said Trumble with a frown at his empty cup, "looks like things are winding down. Better call it a night."

"Thanks for coming." Addie gave him a quick farewell hug. "Say hi to Barb for me. Tell her to stop by the shop when she gets a chance."

"I'll do that. And you be sure to look up Mel at Cove Realty," Trumble told Jack. "He'll find you just what you're looking for."

"Thanks for the tip."

"Mel's a jerk," said Addie after the neighbor had gone.

"Good to know," said Jack.

"You'd have figured it out for yourself in about five minutes. I'm just saving you some time."

"I appreciate it."

Charlie moved past him—her mouth set in a thin, stiff line and resentment rolling off her in waves—to collect empties from the buffet table. "I can use all the help I can get to navigate the waters around this place," he said.

Addie's shoulders lifted and fell with a deep sigh. "Never mind her. She gets this way sometimes. She'll snap out of it."

"I just hope she doesn't snap my head off while she's at it."

"You could tell her I invited you."

"I already did."

Addie waved goodbye to several more guests. "You could tell her—"

"Addie." Jack straightened and took her empty cup. "The guest of honor shouldn't have to think about anything other than enjoying her party. Can I get you another drink?"

Addie's gave him one of her friendliest smiles. "No, thanks. I'm driving myself home."

"If you want a chauffeur, just give a holler."

"You know something, Jack? You're a very nice man." She brushed a casual kiss over his cheek. "Thanks again for my birthday present. That crystal's going to look great dangling above my workbench."

"Glad you like it." He lifted the two empty cups. "Excuse me while I get rid of these."

He made his way to the kitchen, nodding goodbyes to the guests heading in the opposite direction. The crowd was thinning, and someone had turned the sound system volume from ear damaging to loud.

Tess stepped into his path. "I'll take those."

"I thought I'd stick around a while longer," said Jack as he handed them over. "Maybe give you a hand with the cleanup."

"Thanks, but we've got it under control."

"Don't waste your breath on an argument," said Charlie as she squeezed past. "He won't leave until he's good and ready."

"Fine." Tess shoved the cups back into Jack's hands.

"If you're staying, I'm leaving. And I'm taking the birthday girl with me. She's still too young to be exposed to scenes containing adult language and graphic violence."

He moved into the kitchen and scooped paper and plastic trash into the large garbage sack sagging in the corner. When it was filled, he retrieved his jacket from the back bedroom and pulled it on before carrying the trash out to the cans behind Charlie's truck. Hardy danced around his ankles but kept his muddy paws on the ground where they belonged.

Charlie was in the kitchen when he returned, wiping down the counter. Two more bags were sitting by the back door. "Those can wait until morning," she said when he bent to pick them up.

He moved to the sink to wash his hands, and she crossed the room to clean the table, avoiding eye contact. "Tess and Addie told me to tell you goodbye," she said. "Everyone else has left. You can go now, too."

"I was hoping we could talk." He dried his hands with the towel she'd crumpled in an untidy heap and wedged in one corner of the oven door handle. "But if you're too tired, it can wait for morning."

She pulled out a chair and dropped into it with a sigh. "I'm going to have to deal with it eventually. Might as well get it over with."

"You make it sound like I'm a sticky bandage about to be ripped off a wound."

"Yep, that would just about describe it." She rubbed at a crease in the cloth. "I'd offer you some coffee, but there isn't any left."

"I don't need coffee." He neatly folded the towel and looped it over the center of the handle. "And you look like you could use a break from playing the hostess."

"The party was Tess's idea."

"Was it Tess's idea to hold it at your house?"

"Yeah. Well." Charlie shoved her fingers through her hair and let her hands fall into her lap. "What is it you wanted to talk about?"

"You."

"What about me?"

"And me."

"We're not a couple, Jack."

"We could be."

"Impossible."

"Not for us." He straightened away from the counter. "We're good together."

"We've never been together."

"Saying it often enough doesn't always make it so. I've lost count of how many times you've told me I'd leave, and yet I'm still here. Right here, in your kitchen." He joined her at the table. "We've been circling around each other long enough, I think. Circling around business, circling around a relationship. Sooner or later we're going to have to start heading in a straight line."

"What straight line did you have in mind?"

He leaned toward her. "I want you. You know I do."

"That's pretty straightforward, all right."

"And you want me. Admit it."

"You're right," she said with a sigh. "I do. You don't have to beg or do anything else that might embarrass us both."

"And I'm not leaving, Charlie."

"So you say."

"Listen to me." He wrapped his fingers around hers and waited for her to meet his gaze. To face the truth of what they'd shared a few nights ago. "I'm not leaving. I'm not like the other men in your life. I'm not a quitter."

"Funny words from someone who just ditched his job."

"To make a new start, to work for myself. To make a life with roots, Charlie. I'm sticking around, and you're going to have to deal with it."

"If you stick around, Maguire," she said as she twisted from his grip, "if you manage to talk Earl into selling BayRock to you, then that makes you my competitor. And that's the end of this rela—whatever this is."

"That sounds like blackmail."

"It sounds like what it is. The truth."

"Are you suggesting I make a choice between BayRock and you?"

Her laugh was short and hollow. "What kind of a choice is that?"

"You still don't get it, do you?" He shoved away from the table, unable to sit while his frustration edged toward anger. "After the other night—after everything—you can sit there and ask me that?"

He zipped up his jacket. "I thought we'd started something here, Charlie. Something special, something that deserved some care and a chance to grow. But if you still don't understand how I feel about you, about this you-and-me thing, then—"

He bit off his bitter words, knowing he'd never be able

to call them back. "I'm going back to Agatha's. And I have to go back to San Francisco tomorrow to finish things there. And then I'm going to find a Realtor and start looking for a house here in Carnelian Cove. Maybe that little green one down at the end of this street—I noticed there was a For Sale sign out front."

She stood so quickly her chair crashed to the floor. "You wouldn't dare."

"Watch me." He stalked through her house, headed for the front door. Before he reached for the knob, he turned to find her standing in the dining room. "One more thing, Charlie. I was a tough competitor when I was working for Continental. I'm working for myself now. If you thought I was trouble before—watch out."

"That sounded like a threat."

"Good. I wasn't sure you'd pick up on the accent." He stepped out on the front porch.

"You keep saying you care for me." She raced to the open doorway and stood, shivering, in the cold. "If you really cared for me as much as you say you do, you'd quit going after BayRock. You know what it means to me."

"Yeah, I do. But do you know what it means to me?"

She shook her head, her eyes wide and dark against her pale skin.

He muttered an ugly curse. "Figure it out, Charlie."

CHAPTER NINETEEN

JACK'S PHONE WAS RINGING when he stepped into his San Francisco office Monday morning. "Maguire."

"Jack, it's Agatha."

His grip tightened on the receiver at the solemn tone of her voice. Bad news. "Hello, Agatha."

"I apologize for calling you at work, but I thought you'd want to know. Earl Sawyer's brother passed away yesterday. He's already left for Oregon to attend the funeral."

Jack closed his eyes and lowered his head. "I didn't know he had a brother."

"Few of us did. They weren't very close."

"Does Charlie know?"

"I'm sure she does. It was Maudie who called me with the news."

Maudie Keene. Interesting. "When is he due back?"

"The middle of the week. I'm not sure when, exactly."

"I'd like to come up and give my condolences in person." And though it wasn't the best time to talk business, Jack preferred to do that in person, too. "Will you do me a favor and call me when he shows up again?"

ON WEDNESDAY EVENING, JACK walked into The Shantyman and headed for one of the small tables arranged along the wall.

"Hello, Earl."

"Jack." Sawyer squinted at him for a long moment, and then reached across the table to shake his hand. "Thanks for the invitation. I appreciate the gesture."

"You're welcome." He pulled out a chair and joined Sawyer, who, judging from the evidence of his red-rimmed eyes and the empty glass on the table, had started without him. "My condolences."

Sawyer grunted in acknowledgment.

"I'm glad you agreed to join me." Jack signaled for service. "Did you have a wake for your brother in Oregon?"

"Nope." Sawyer frowned. "My sister-in-law doesn't approve of that kind of thing."

"Well, we Irish happen to think a wake is a matter of the utmost necessity."

"You offering to buy me a drink?" asked Sawyer as the waiter appeared.

"I'm offering to buy you as many as you want. It's the reason I came all this way."

They gave their orders, and Jack opened a tab.

"Agatha says you brought your car up and left it here. Nice car, from what I hear."

Jack grinned. "I like it."

"I always wanted a hot car like that." Sawyer shrugged. "Always wanted a lot of things."

"You'll have them someday." Jack leaned his elbows

on the table. "And someday soon you'll have the time to enjoy them."

"That kind of time would be nice to have." Sawyer's squinty stare softened around the edges. "Life's too short."

"Yes, it is." Their drinks were served, and Jack lifted his glass. "To quality of life. May we always choose the very best for ourselves and never take it for granted."

Sawyer hefted his frosted mug with a grunt and took a large swig of his beer.

Someone started up the jukebox, and the floor throbbed in time to the bass. A couple of college-age customers started a pool game with a lot of chalk and swagger.

"Charlie would never make me an offer like that," said Sawyer.

"What offer?"

"To buy me as many drinks as I wanted."

"No, I don't s'pose she would." Jack's lips twitched at the idea. "Doesn't sound like her style."

"Hell, even if she did, I wouldn't take her up on it," said Sawyer. "We don't get along all that well."

Jack nodded philosophically. "She can be a difficult woman."

"You seem to like her well enough."

"Yes. Yes, I do."

Sawyer leaned in close. "Bet she'll be hot as a pistol if she finds out about this discussion."

"She'll get over it."

"Never met a man like you, Jack." Sawyer slapped him on the shoulder hard enough to make Jack wince. "Never knew anyone who could make so much trouble for himself and still manage to be so cheerful about it."

"Like you said, Earl, life's too short." Jack sipped his whiskey. "I figure it's too short for dwelling on problems. Easier to solve them, or ignore them and move on."

"Damn right."

Earl drained his glass and signaled for another. Too many more, and Jack wouldn't feel right introducing the topic he'd hoped to discuss.

He cleared his throat. "I know I said I wasn't going to talk business tonight, but I'm thinking about my promise to give you a firm commitment by Monday and the schedule facing me when I get back. And how much you wanted to tie this up fast."

"Yeah." Sawyer stared into his mug. "Like I said, life's too short. I want to retire while I can still enjoy it."

"And that's one of the reasons I hope you'll listen to my offer."

Sawyer gave him a long, squinty stare. "Okay," he said with a nod. "I'm listening."

Jack leaned in close. "I'm in. But not for an auction. I'll make my offer, and that's that. I'm open to negotiating terms of the related arrangements, not a series of bids to ratchet up the price."

"Hmm." Sawyer scrubbed his fingers through his beard. "Guess I can see your point about wanting to avoid another round or two with Charlie."

Jack gave him a faint smile. "She's a scrapper."

"She sure is."

"But she'll be wanting to avoid that kind of a round with

me, too. She can't afford it, and I don't want to waste the time." Jack leaned back and crossed his ankle over his knee. "I want to settle this thing, soon as I can. I think that's best, for everyone involved."

"Maybe I want a little time to give another interested party a chance to put in a bid of their own."

"If you're looking in Continental's direction, you're going to be disappointed. This deal was mine to make. I tried, and I failed. It happens," added Jack when he noted the skeptical look on the older man's face. "Not often, but it does. And that's no bluff."

Sawyer frowned. "Continental's not the only player in this part of the country."

"True. But it's the elephant in the room. The fact that Continental was up here sniffing around might mean it'll come back later, maybe cause some trouble. Or it might mean there's nothing here worth the effort."

They paused while the waiter delivered Sawyer's refill. Sawyer picked up his mug and regarded Jack over the rim. "Sounds like an excuse to lower the asking price."

"It's a mighty rickety piece of leverage, considering I'm the one who did the sniffing. Besides," added Jack with a smile, "you've got some leverage of your own. Up to a point, anyway."

"Charlie."

"That's right. My competition." Jack's gut tightened and his smile faded. He thought he'd stowed all his nerves and guilt before he'd launched this discussion. "She can't afford to go too high, and I can't afford to go too low, not if I want to stay in the game. And I do."

Sawyer lifted his beer to his lips. "Sounds like we all ended up right back where we started."

"Happens that way sometimes."

Jack sat very still, waiting for Sawyer to make the next move. He'd had his say, and he didn't want to muddy up the moment. He donned his poker face and directed his gaze toward the television screen to make the waiting easier on them both.

"Well?" asked Sawyer.

"Well, what?"

"Aren't you going to make your offer?"

"Yeah." He named a figure and watched for the tells. There they were—the tiny tug at one corner of Sawyer's mouth and a faint, calculating squint around his eyes. The rest of the discussion, about the payment schedule and taxes and consulting fees, would be fairly routine.

BayRock was his.

CHAPTER TWENTY

WHEN THE BELL ABOVE THE museum's entrance jangled early Wednesday morning, Maudie stepped into the main room, feather duster in hand, to see a tall, handsome stranger waiting near the reception counter.

Jack Maguire. Geneva's description had been detailed and flawless, right down to the gorgeous grooves bracketing his mouth. She took a deep breath and prepared to deal with whatever this visit would bring. "May I help you?"

"I s'pose that depends on whether or not I have the pleasure of addressing Maudie Keene."

"I don't know whether it's a pleasure, Mr. Maguire, but yes, I'm Maudie."

That amazing smile of his widened until it seemed to light all the dark, musty corners of the displays, and she struggled against the urge to smile back. What a charmer. No wonder her daughter hadn't been able to withstand the full force of this man's attentions.

"I'm going to feel at a disadvantage," he said, "if I'm to call you Maudie while you're calling me mister."

She smiled politely. "What can I do for you, Jack?"

"I have to admit I've been asking myself the same thing since I walked in that door. And I'm still not sure I know the answer to the question." He shoved his hands into his pockets. "I guess I'm going to feel at a disadvantage no matter what we call each other."

She set the duster on a large glass case. "Would you care for a cup of coffee, Jack?"

"Yes, I would, thank you."

He followed her to the tiny employee lounge near the rear exit and waited at the door while she filled two foam cups. "How do you take it?"

"Black," he said. "Thank you."

"You may as well come in and have a seat," she said as she handed him his cup. "I rarely get visitors in the middle of the week, and if anyone comes in, we'll be able to hear the bell."

"All right." He waited until she'd settled in one of the plastic chairs and then he took the other, folding his long legs beneath him and shifting his knees to the side in the cramped space.

"You're taller than I'd expected," she said.

"And you're younger-looking."

"Thank you."

A silence stretched between them, surprising her. She'd been told the Southerner was a real talker. "I could ask what your intentions are," she said, "and let you decide which situation to discuss first."

"That would be one way to get this conversation started." He stared at his coffee and then at her. "One of my intentions is to avoid causing any member of the Keene family any distress over business matters during the next few weeks."

"You make it sound as though you think that's inevitable."

"I don't believe it is," he said, shaking his head. "It doesn't have to be."

"Would the reason you stopped by this morning have something to do with avoiding that inevitability?"

He grinned. "I'd heard your daughter takes after you."

"Do you think so?" The idea—and his obvious enjoyment of it—pleased her.

"I think Charlie has a ways to go before she learns how to be direct and discreet at the same time," he said.

"Subtlety has never been her strong suit."

"No, ma'am."

"But you like that about her."

"Yes, I do." He shifted in his chair. "There are a great many things I like about your daughter."

"I'm glad to hear it." She wondered if she could trust this man to be direct and discreet. "I wouldn't want my daughter getting involved with a man who didn't appreciate her enough to accept the flaws that come with the package."

"You needn't worry about me or my intentions toward your daughter, Maudie."

She set her coffee aside and spread her hands on the little table. "I was told you're a smooth talker, Jack. A clever businessman and a skilled deal maker. But you can't negotiate or finesse your way through this. If you care for Charlie at all, you must know she'll want straight talk."

"Oh, I've done all the straight talking I care to at this point. And I've discovered that the problem with being so up-front about things is it doesn't leave much in the way of a fallback position."

He leveled a calm, cool, businesslike gaze at her. "The

way I see it, there's only one chance for working out a compromise. And that involves you, Maudie."

"YOUR MOTHER WANTS TO SEE YOU," said Gus when Charlie walked into the Keene office Wednesday afternoon.

"Did she finish with those DMV forms already?" Charlie sighed and shook her head. "She works so fast, I can't keep up with her."

"Never thought I'd hear that complaint around here," said Gus.

"Who's complaining?" Charlie smiled. "I think she deserves a promotion. What title haven't we used yet?"

She headed down the hall toward David's office, her mother's temporary work space, and poked her head inside the open door. "Mom?"

"Oh, hello, Charlie." Maudie brushed her hair out of her eyes and settled back in the tall desk chair. "Come on in."

Charlie took a seat, rubbing her hands over her jeans. "What's up?"

"I had a talk with Jack Maguire this morning."

Charlie dug her fingernails into her palms, trying to focus on the pain in her hands instead of the pressure on her heart. "He called?"

"He's here."

Charlie wiped the frown from her face. No emotion. Nothing personal. Strictly business. "What did he want?"

"To meet me, I think." Maudie tapped a pencil against the desk blotter. "You're not upset, are you?"

"Why would I be upset?"

"Because you're in love with him."

Charlie straightened in her seat, so tense she wondered if her mother could see her vibrate. "That has nothing to do with anything."

"I think it has a great deal to do with a great many things, including your future."

"He has no place in that."

"Charlie." Maudie threw down the pencil. "Don't blow this. Please."

"I'm not planning on it."

"He loves you."

"He said that?"

"He didn't have to," said Maudie, smiling. "It's clear as can be."

"He hasn't said anything about that."

"Have you asked him?"

Charlie crossed her arms with a scowl. "Why would I do that?"

"To give him the chance to tell you." Her mother rose from her chair and brushed her hand over her trendy knit dress. "Have you told him how you feel?"

"And let him use it against me in a business deal?"

Maudie frowned. "If that's what you think, then I feel sorry for both of you."

She pulled her sweater from David's rack and draped it over her arm. "I have an appointment. I'll talk to you later."

Charlie slumped in her seat after her mother left, allowing herself to wallow in self-pity for a minute. Or two.

The desk phone buzzed, and Charlie punched the button to connect with dispatch. "Sawyer, line one," said Gus. "And Maguire, line two."

She tightened her fingers on the receiver. What were the odds of them both calling at exactly the same time? "I'll take the call from Sawyer. Tell Maguire my mother's gone for the day."

"Doesn't matter," said Gus. "He wants to talk to you, too."

JACK STROLLED INTO HIS favorite coffee shop shortly after Mona opened the door for business on Thursday morning and paused to admire the painting of *Carmona Miranda* hanging above the cash register.

"It's new," said Mona as she handed him his usual espresso with a shot of vanilla.

"That's a good spot for it." He wondered what da Vinci might have thought of Mona's arching black brows, cherry-red lips and fruit-loaded turban. "Brightens up the place."

"I agree. Put up another new one in the back corner over the weekend. *Mona Cubed.*"

"Let me guess," said Jack with a smile. "Picasso?"

"Got to love a man who understands the finer things in life." She poured a cup of chai tea for herself and leaned on the counter. "It's an early cubist style, so you can still see the likeness. Someone brought in one of those more abstract versions last year. I liked it, but it could have been anyone."

"Can't have that."

"No indeed. Got to stick with my theme." Mona blew on her tea. "You're up early."

"I've got a business meeting. I wanted your finest corner

table, and I figured I'd have to get here at the crack of dawn to stake my claim." He tasted his espresso. "Do you know Charlie Keene?"

"I know a David Keene."

"Her brother."

"He's got a good eye," said Mona. "Real talent."

"Is that right?"

"He showed me a sketch for a Mona sculpture, but I told him I was sticking with the paintings. Charlie Keene." Mona sipped and considered. "Short woman? Red hair?"

"That's her." Jack pulled another bill from his wallet. "She's my business appointment. Give her anything she wants, add on my usual to-go order, and keep the change."

Mona's eyebrows shot up. "Unless she wants most of what's inside my pastry case, that's going to be a big chunk of change."

"I might be taking up that back corner table for a while, depending on the business."

"Doesn't mean you have to pay a month's rent."

Jack tucked *The Cove Press* beneath one arm and carried his cup to his favorite spot by the window. He settled into the chair facing the shop entrance and opened the paper to the real estate section. Framed in the window, a fishing boat motored out of the marina, slicing through the layer of mist hovering over the rippling water. Over Jack's shoulder, *Mona Cubed* stared down her sharp pink nose with one flat black eye.

Five minutes later he'd rejected several decent housing prospects, and he refolded the paper and set it aside with a frown. He already knew where he wanted to live—and with whom.

Charlie's mud-spattered pickup pulled to the curb near one of the docks. A moment later she stepped to the pavement, slammed her truck door and jaywalked toward the shop. She nearly stumbled over the curb when she spied him grinning at her through the window, and she froze, just for a moment, while hot spots reddened her cheeks. And then her eyes—Jack knew they were as dark and gray as the bay water—narrowed to slits, and a touch of that heat she could generate snapped and sizzled right through him.

He rubbed a fist over his heart. God almighty, he loved that flamethrower stare of hers.

"Thank you for coming." He stood and pulled out a chair for her as she neared his table.

"You didn't leave me much choice in the matter."

"I don't want you to feel that way. Especially not this morning."

"Guess you'll just have to deal with it." She lifted her chin and looked him straight in the eye. "Congratulations on the BayRock deal."

"Thank you."

He waited patiently until she took her seat, and he bit back a grin at her huge sigh when he fussed with her chair.

"Well, what is it?" she asked. "Why did you drag me down here?"

"I have a proposition for you." He waited a beat, but she didn't so much as bat an eyelash. "A business proposition."

"Okay. Shoot."

"Continental's still out there. My soon-to-be former assistant, Sally, has all my reports. All my data on the local supply, among other things. After she gets that promotion I figure she's got coming, I'd give her all of five minutes before she heads this way, looking to make a deal."

"So deal." Charlie shot him a dark look. "Or I will."

"You would? With Continental?"

"Or whoever shows up." She dropped her sprinkle-covered doughnut and shifted forward. "You've given me a lot to think about during the past couple of weeks. And some of the things I thought I knew for sure turned out to be different than what I'd been thinking all along."

He studied her features, searching for some clue to the emotions beneath her deadpan delivery. "But not everything," he said at last.

"No." She shrugged. "Some things never change."

"Like the way you feel about Keene Concrete." He tried to keep the question out of his voice, but it snuck in, weak and wobbly.

She shrugged again as she reached for the sugar, and he was tempted to reach across the table, grab her by the scruff of her grimy denim jacket and haul her into his lap.

Instead, he stretched his legs out into the aisle, crossing them at the ankles. "I think we should look for a way to join forces. Merge the two companies in a fashion that would benefit all the owners—those who want to stay and those who want to leave. Make it easier to fend off any unwanted buyout offers from larger outfits."

She stopped stirring her coffee and glanced up. "How would we go about doing this?"

"We'd form a new corporation. A new business identity. One that would allow us to remain as independent as each of us wishes while taking advantage of whatever resources we decide to share."

"What exactly are you talking about here, Jack?"

"I told you." He cleared his throat. "A business proposition."

"And is that your only proposition? A suggestion to form a new corporation?"

He met her steady gaze and swallowed. "Yes."

"Just business, right? Nothing personal."

"That's right."

She slapped her palms on the table and shoved to her feet. "Damn you."

"What?"

"I said, *damn you*."

"Now, Charlie—"

She leaned over him. "Just business, right? Nothing personal, hmm? Well, what if I want things between us to be personal—what about that? How are you going to figure that equation into the new corporate structure, Mr. Call-Me-Jack Maguire?"

She turned on her boot heel and stormed out of the shop.

"Better go after her," said Mona, handing him his little white take-out bag as he dashed past her.

"Don't worry," said Jack at the door. "We're not finished." *Not by a long shot.*

He ran out and caught up with her near the foot of *D*

dock. Behind her, Crazy Ed reeled in his line and headed their way.

"Charlie. Wait up." Jack took her by the arm and spun her around. "I wasn't finished back there."

She tugged herself free of his grasp. "Make it fast. I've got a business to run."

"All right." He cleared his throat. "You asked how I thought I might figure a personal equation into the corporate structure. Well, I s'pose I could ask you to marry me, if I didn't think I might get my head bitten off and handed to me in the process."

"Chicken, Maguire?"

"Damn straight." He glared at her. "I—"

"Hey, Jack." Ed shuffled from foot to foot, eyeing the bag in Jack's hand. "Gonna come fishing with me this afternoon?"

Jack handed him the bag. "This isn't a good time, Ed. Can we talk later?"

"Sure, buddy." Ed pulled out a doughnut and gave him a gap-toothed grin. "Glazed. My favorite."

"Don't give it all to the gulls."

Jack patted him on the arm and turned back to Charlie. She was staring at him with a soft smile. "You know Crazy Ed," she said.

"Yeah, we've met."

"No. I mean, you *know* him. Don't you?"

"Yeah, sure. He used to be a postal clerk in Modesto. Right, Ed?"

A few doughnut crumbs leaked out of the edges of Ed's smile.

"And he knows you," said Charlie.

"Yeah, I guess so. We don't talk about me much, and I'm not sure how much he'd remember, to tell the truth. Besides, I like listening to his stories."

She crossed her arms. "Go ahead. Ask me."

"What did you say?"

"I said, ask me to marry you."

"Here? Now?" Jack frowned. "Because of Crazy Ed?"

"That's right." Her smile widened. "Because you really are a friendly guy. And I love you, so I'd be crazy to say no."

Jack caught her by her jacket and pulled her close, and the feel of her against him was perfect—just the right combination of sugar and spice. Exactly the right woman for him. "I love you, Charlie."

"Glad to hear it."

"I love you, too," said Ed.

"Go away, Ed," said Jack.

Charlie buried her face against Jack's sweatshirt, her shoulders shaking.

Jack waited for Ed to wander to the end of the dock. "Sorry. This isn't the most romantic setting for a business proposition."

Charlie tipped her head back and met his gaze. "Did you think I needed that?"

"No." He kissed the tip of her nose. "I think you need me."

"Friendly *and* smart. Quite a bargain."

"Marry me, and you can have both for the price of one."

"Okay," said Charlie, and she balanced on the toes of her boots to give him a kiss that was her own sweet version of paradise. "It's a deal."

* * * * *

Mills & Boon® Special Moments™
brings you a sneak preview…

*Turn the page for a peek at this fantastic new
story from Victoria Pade, available next
month in Mills & Boon!*

*When Tate McCord caught reporter Tanya Kimbrough
snooping around the McCord mansion for business
secrets, he had to admit – the housekeeper's daughter
had become a knockout! The real scoop – this Texas
Cinderella was about to steal the surgeon's heart.*

Texas Cinderella
by
Victoria Pade

"**S**ometimes I don't understand you, Blake. You open up enough to let me know the business is in a slump, that you think we really can find the Santa Magdalena diamond and use it to pull us out of the fire. But you bite off my head for asking how things are going."

Tanya Kimbrough froze.

It was nearly eleven o'clock on Friday night and she had no business doing what she was doing in the library of the Dallas mansion of the family her mother worked for. But her mother had gone to bed and Tanya had known the McCords were all at a charity symphony that should have kept them out much later than this. And she'd gotten nosy.

But now here she was, overhearing the raised voice of Tate McCord as he and his older brother came into the formal living room that was just beyond the library. The library where she'd turned on the overhead lights because she'd thought she would be in and out long before any of the McCords got home…

Make a run for it the way you came in, she advised herself.

She certainly couldn't turn off the library lights without drawing attention since the doors to the living room were ajar. But maybe Tate and Blake McCord would only think someone had forgotten to turn them off before they'd left the house tonight. And if she went out the way she'd come in, no one would guess that she'd used her mother's keys to let herself in through the French doors that opened to the rear grounds of the sprawling estate. If she just left right now…

But then Blake McCord answered his brother and she stayed where she was. What she was listening to suited her purposes so much better than what she'd already found on the library desk.

"Finding the Santa Magdalena and buying up canary diamonds for a related jewelry line are in the works," Blake was saying. "And we've launched the initial Once In A Lifetime promotional campaign in the stores to pamper customers and bring in more business. That's all you have to know since you—and everyone else—are on a need-to-know-only basis. Your time and interest might be better spent paying some attention to your fiancée, wouldn't you say?"

"What I'd say is that *that* isn't any of your business," Tate answered in a tone that surprised Tanya.

The sharp edge coming from Tate didn't sound anything like him. The brothers generally got along well, and Tate had always been the easygoing brother. Tanya's mother had said that Tate had changed since spending a year working in the Middle East and suddenly Tanya didn't doubt it.

"It may not be my business, but I'm telling you anyway because someone has to," Blake persisted. "You take Katie for granted, you neglect her, you don't pay her nearly enough attention. You may think you have her all sewed up with that engagement ring on her finger, but if you don't start giving her some indication that you know she's alive, she could end up throwing it in your face. And nobody would blame her if she did."

Katie was Katerina Whitcomb-Salgar, the daughter of the McCord family's longtime friends and the woman everyone had always assumed would end up as Mrs. Tate McCord long before their formal engagement was announced.

"You're going to lose Katie," Blake shouted, some heat in his voice now. "And if you do, it'll serve you right."

"Or it might be for the best," Tate countered, enough under his breath that Tanya barely made out what he'd said. Then more loudly again, he added, "Just keep your eye on finding that diamond and getting McCord's Jewelers and the family coffers healthy again. Since you want to carry all the weight for that yourself, you shouldn't have a lot of spare time to worry about my love life, too. But if I want your advice, I'll be sure to ask for it."

"You need someone's advice or you're going to blow the best thing that ever happened to you."

"Thanks for the heads-up," Tate said facetiously.

And then there were footsteps.

But only some of them moved away from the library.

The others were coming closer...

Too late to run.

Tanya ducked for cover, hoping that since she was behind the desk whoever was headed her way wouldn't be able to see her when he reached in and turned off the lights.

"Tate hasn't even been staying in the house since he got back. He's living in the guest cottage..."

Tanya's mother's words flashed through her mind just then and it struck her that merely having the lights turned off might not be what was about to happen. That Tate might use the library route to go to the guesthouse that was also out back....

Tanya's heart had begun to race the minute she'd heard the McCords' voices. Now it was pounding. Because while she might have been able to explain her presence in the library at this time of night, how would she ever explain crouching behind the desk?

Or holding the papers she'd been looking through—because until that minute she hadn't even realized she'd taken them with her when she'd ducked.

Please don't come in here....

"What the hell?"

Oh, no...

Tanya had tried to turn herself into a small ball but when Tate McCord's voice boomed from nearby, she raised her head to find him leaning over the front of the desk, clearly able to see her.

This was much, much worse than when she was six and had been caught with her fingers in the icing of his twin sisters' birthday cake. His mother Eleanor had been kind and understanding. But there was nothing kind or understanding in Tate McCord's face at that moment.

Summoning what little dignity she could—and with the papers still in hand—Tanya stood.

It was the first time she and Tate McCord had set eyes on each other in the seven years since Tanya had left for college. And even before that—when Tate had come home from his own university and medical school training for vacations or visits while Tanya still lived on the property with her mother—there weren't many occasions when the McCord heir had crossed paths with the housekeeper's daughter. Plus, Tanya had been very well aware of the fact that, more often than not, when any of the McCords had seen her, they'd looked through her rather than at her.

So she wasn't sure Tate McCord recognized her and, as if it would make this better, she said, "You probably don't remember me—"

"You're JoBeth's daughter—Tanya," he said bluntly. "What the hell are you doing in here at this hour and—"

He glanced down at the papers and held out his hand in a silent demand for her to give them to him.

TEXAS CINDERELLA *by Victoria Pade*

A hidden diamond and a dramatic feud! Will Tate be able to keep his
family secrets from sassy journalist Tanya, even as he falls in love?

THE TEXAS CEO'S SECRET *by Nicole Foster*

Katerina and Blake were meant to be friends, linked by marriage –
but not to each other. But a passionate kiss changes everything.

STAR-CROSSED SWEETHEARTS *by Jackie Braun*

Hiding from the press in Italy, actress Atlanta wants to be alone.
Will former bad boy Angelo show her that the limelight is fleeting
and it's family and love that count?

SECRET PRINCE, INSTANT DADDY! *by Raye Morgan*

When pretty Ayme tracks him down, deposed royal Darius, sure he is the
father of her late sister's baby, must decide how he can fulfil his destiny
and find his own happiness.

AT HOME IN STONE CREEK *by Linda Lael Miller*

Everyone in Ashley 's life is marrying and starting families. Now Jack,
the man who broke her heart years ago, is back. But is he who she
thinks he is?

Cherish™

On sale from 17th September 2010
Don't miss out!

Available at WHSmith, Tesco, ASDA, Eason
and all good bookshops

www.millsandboon.co.uk

A MIRACLE FOR HIS SECRET SON
by Barbara Hannay

Freya never intended Gus to find out about their son. But when young
Nick needs a kidney transplant she tracks him down. Could this be
their chance to be a family?

PROUD RANCHER, PRECIOUS BUNDLE
by Donna Alwood

Wyatt and Elli have already had a run-in. But when a baby is left on
his doorstep, Wyatt needs help. Will romance between them flare as
they care for baby Darcy?

ACCIDENTALLY PREGNANT!
by Rebecca Winters

Left pregnant and alone, Irena is determined to keep her baby a secret.
Can Vincenzo, the man she had a passionate affair with, give her the
love she needs?

2 FREE BOOKS
AND A SURPRISE GIFT

We would like to take this opportunity to thank you for reading this Mills & Boon® book by offering you the chance to take TWO more specially selected books from the Special Moments™ series absolutely FREE! We're also making this offer to introduce you to the benefits of the Mills & Boon® Book Club™—

- **FREE home delivery**
- **FREE gifts and competitions**
- **FREE monthly Newsletter**
- **Exclusive Mills & Boon Book Club offers**
- **Books available before they're in the shops**

Accepting these FREE books and gift places you under no obligation to buy, you may cancel at any time, even after receiving your free books. Simply complete your details below and return the entire page to the address below. You don't even need a stamp!

YES Please send me 2 free Special Moments books and a surprise gift. I understand that unless you hear from me, I will receive 5 superb new stories every month, including a 2-in-1 book priced at £4.99 and three single books priced at £3.19 each, postage and packing free. I am under no obligation to purchase any books and may cancel my subscription at any time. The free books and gift will be mine to keep in any case.

Ms/Mrs/Miss/Mr _____ Initials _____

_____

Surname _____

Address _____

_____

_____ Postcode _____

E-mail _____

Send this whole page to: Mills & Boon Book Club, Free Book Offer, FREEPOST NAT 10298, Richmond, TW9 1BR